Fixtures & Fittings

Julia Blake

copyright ©Julia Blake 2017
All rights reserved

Sele Books
www.selebooks.com

This is a work of fiction. All characters and events in this publication, other than those in the public domain, are either a product of the author's imagination or are used in a fictitious manner. Any resemblance to actual persons, living or dead, or actual events is purely coincidental.

No part of this publication may be reproduced, distributed, or transmitted in any form or by any means, without the written permission of the author, except in the case of brief quotations embodied in critical reviews and certain other non-commercial uses permitted by copyright law.

For permission requests contact the author.

www.juliablakeauthor.co.uk

ISBN 9781981321780

Fixtures & Fittings is written in British English and has an estimated UK cinema rating of 12+ containing mild violence, occasional bad language and mild sexual references

Fixtures & Fittings is an Authors Alike accredited book

~Dedication~

To my parents, as ever, thank you

To all my social media family who cheered me on my mad quest to write a book in a fortnight, offering support and much-needed encouragement, thank you

~ Acknowledgements ~

A big thank you, as ever to my wonderful editor Dani. Thanks, missy, you're a stern taskmaster but I wouldn't have you any other way.

Thanks, must also go to my eagle-eyed beta readers, Caroline Noe, and Trisha J. Kelly. Both talented authors, you can find them at:

carolinenoe.org
facebook.com/TrishajkellyAuthor/

Finally, a massive thank you to James and Becky Wright at Platform House Publishing for all their patient help with formatting and all their advice and creative input with the fabulous cover and interior graphics. Thanks, guys, you are amazing.

For all your publishing needs, contact Becky at:

www.platformhousepublishing.co.uk

~A Note for the Reader~

After the success of Lost & Found, I had so many readers contact me wanting to know more about the Blackwood family, begging for more stories.

Fixtures & Fittings follows straight on from Lost & Found and is Marcus's story. Successful, handsome, and rich, Marcus ends up with more on his plate than he ever expected and has met his match in single mum, Grace Lovejoy.

As always, you can contact me on:
Facebook: Julia Blake Author
Instagram: @juliablakeauthor

And you can read all about my crazy life on my weekly blog "A Little Bit of Blake" on

https://juliablakeauthor.home.blog

You can also find out all about me and my books on my website:

www.juliablakeauthor.co.uk

~ The Blackwood Family ~

ONE
Legend of a Man

THREE
Very Different Wives

SIX
Individual Children

SEVEN
Extraordinary Tales

This is...

*THE
BLACKWOOD
FAMILY SAGA*

~A Family History ~

The Blackwoods are a wonderful, eccentric, rambling family. To quote Luke Blackwood – "they might be a hotchpotch of exes, steps and halves, but they're my family and I love them."

Originally founded by George Blackwood, a legendary fighter of a man, he and his first wife Celeste built a business empire between them and had two children, Monica and Marcus. But pressure soon split the perfect family cleanly down the middle with Celeste returning to her native New York and taking Monica with her, Marcus remaining in Britain to be raised by his father to take over the business one day.

George then fell immediately into another marriage with Marina, and for a while, things looked to be going his way, especially with the rapid arrival of their two children Luke and Susannah. However, George was soon left heartbroken when this marriage also disintegrated, with Marina stating she would always love him but could no longer stand the pace of his life and of always coming second to his business. The pair remained firm friends, Marina even taking on the upbringing of George's eldest son, Marcus.

Alone and working too hard, the inevitable happened and George was hospitalised following a heart attack. Regaining consciousness after surgery, the first thing George saw were the laughing green eyes of his Irish nurse, Siobhan.

Two months later the pair were married, and despite the thirty years age difference between them, were blissfully happy for ten years, during which time Siobhan bore him two children, a son called Liam and a daughter called Kristina (Kit).

The whole family were devastated though when George, by then in his late sixties, suffered another heart attack and died, leaving behind three women who had all loved him passionately in their own ways, six children and one granddaughter, Megan, the child of his eldest daughter, Monica.

He also left behind a sizeable legacy to be split evenly between them, a multi-million pound business empire now ably run by his eldest son, Marcus, and a deep-seated work ethic tempered by bone-deep integrity and a sense of morality.

So that's the state of affairs in the Blackwood family at the beginning of this series. None of the children is yet married, except for Monica, a real estate agent in New York, and Luke. You can read the story of how Luke met the love of his life, Arianna, in Lost & Found, book one of the Blackwood family saga. Marcus is a business tycoon and much sought after social batchelor. Susannah owns a quirky little bookshop. Liam is a war photographer, and Kit is an up and coming opera singer.

All are happy and settled in his or her life, and each has no idea of the adventures they are about to embark on.

Fixtures & Fittings

Book 2 of the
Blackwood Family Saga

Julia Blake

~Chapter One~
"Just come, Marcus, please, just come."

Marcus Blackwood had discovered it was entirely possible for him to fall asleep with his eyes open.

So gifted had he become at this skill that he was able to completely convince the person he was talking to that he was awake, lucid, and giving his whole attention to the matter in hand, when in fact, Marcus was drifting away in a land which existed nowhere else but inside his head.

This talent had saved his sanity during many a long meeting, and as the head of acquisitions and mergers regurgitated an incomprehensible wedge of facts, figures, and forecasts in a monotonous and, dare Marcus even think it, downright boring voice, he could feel his grip on reality beginning to slip.

Sitting bolt upright in his incredibly uncomfortable chair, Marcus blinked several times in a desperate attempt to focus on what was probably very important information.

However, his thoughts were reluctant to obey. Sulky and truculent, they whined and complained about being forced to waste their precious time on such rubbish.

Pay attention, Marcus ordered himself. It was no good. With all the wild enthusiasm of boisterous puppies, his thoughts slipped from his grasp and frisked away into the distance, eager to explore and see what was over the hill.

It didn't help that it was a hot and sticky day. The golden eye of the late afternoon sun streaming through shut windows boiling its occupants, as sluggish air conditioning fought to deal with such an unusually warm British May.

Was it any wonder Marcus's imaginings longed to be anywhere but here? Longed to be somewhere cool and shady where he could relax, loosen his tie, and slip off his tight, patent leather shoes in which his toes squirmed in sweaty, cramped misery.

"Don't you agree, Marcus?"

Marcus blinked, instantly back in the room, realising for once his skill had let him down. He paused, hoping inspiration would strike, unwilling to let his colleagues know he wasn't listening. That all their carefully prepared reports and flow charts had been for nothing because the boss had been asleep.

Eight pairs of expectant slightly sycophantic eyes gazed at him.

A sheen of panic glazed his forehead and Marcus knew he had to say something. He had a fifty-fifty chance of getting it right and hell, even if he got it wrong no one was going to argue with the boss.

'That's a complex question, Nigel," he stalled, and Nigel nodded seriously, myopic gaze blinking behind thick lenses.

"And one that needs a good deal of consideration." Marcus prayed Nigel hadn't asked if it was time to stop for coffee.

His intercom buzzed.

Thankfully, he lunged at it, deciding even though he'd told his PA not to allow any calls through, she deserved a raise.

"Yes?"

"Marcus, you have a call on line one."

Sally's voice was low with concern. Marcus frowned at the taut worry he heard in her tone.

"I did say no calls, Sally," he chided, mildly.

"I know, but I think you need to take this one. Marcus, it's your mother..."

"My mother?"

Marcus shifted in surprise, intensely aware of eight pairs of eyes all busily pretending not to be eavesdropping.

"Yes, your mother," continued Sally. "Something's happened, Marcus, and I think you should talk to her alone."

Marcus's brows flew up in surprise.

Sally had been his PA for many years and was fully aware of his feelings concerning his mother. He knew she'd never normally interrupt a meeting with one of his mother's self-imposed crisis calls.

If Sally said it was important; it was important.

"Right," he said slowly. "Put it through to my office and tell her to hang on, I'll take it there. Oh, and Sally, perhaps you could organise some coffee for everyone?"

"Of course, Marcus."

Marcus hung up and looked around the desk.

"If we could have a ten-minute break, I'll take this call and then we can resume."

There was a general round of agreement. A feeling of relaxation descended over the table as people visibly stood down.

Pushing back chairs and stretching, they looked with anticipation towards the door. It was well known that Marcus's PA supplied the best coffee, and sometimes even brought in homemade cookies.

Closing his office door firmly behind him, Marcus took a second to settle into his leather chair, closing his eyes briefly and letting out a sigh as he prepared to deal with his mother.

It wasn't that he didn't love her. Of course, he did, she was his mother. It was more that he didn't understand her.

Maybe it was the fact she was so very American that sometimes made Marcus feel they came from different planets.

Marcus was British, that was how he viewed himself. Despite his mother being American, despite having a dual nationality passport, as far as Marcus was concerned, he was British as his father had been, British through and through.

His parents had enjoyed a surprisingly happy marriage, but his mother hated Britain and his father couldn't stand America.

When they finally decided to amicably separate, their solution had been to split the family neatly down the middle.

Marcus remained in Britain with his father, attending a good public school where he made the necessary connections to enable him to work his way up the ranks in the family business, before taking over following his father's death.

During the holidays he visited his mother and older sister in America, except at Christmas when they all came back to Britain. Then his mother would throw herself into the festivities, declaring it was so good to be back with her family and this time they would stay.

But by the first week in January, she was itching to return to her friends and her charity work, to the throbbing, bustling metropolis of New York, his mother's natural habitat.

Like a fish out of water, Marcus could see her visibly gasping to breathe its polluted air again. He had accepted early on that this was the way they did things in his family.

Living with his father and his second wife, Marina, Marcus had been delighted to have a new brother and sister to keep him company, the three half-siblings forming a bond as close as any full-blooded family.

His half-brother, Luke, being only four years younger than himself, became Marcus's special confidante. Given the continued absence of his older sister Monica and how like his mother she was, Marcus was closer to Luke than her.

Thinking now of his father, Marcus sighed again, unwilling to admit how much he missed him. Since his death, Marcus had been the one to deal with his mother's habitual phone calls about everything and nothing.

Assuming the mantle of arbitrator and advisor, his mother instead called on him to seek his opinion on every minute detail of her, in Marcus's opinion anyway, shallow existence. Bracing himself, he picked up the phone.

"Mother?"

"Marcus, oh thank god, Marcus, the most terrible thing has happened..."

"Calm down, Mother, take a deep breath and tell me what's wrong."

"Oh, Marcus!"

His mother's sobs echoed down the line with chilling clarity.

Marcus straightened in his chair. This wasn't his mother's normal, fluttering panic, this was genuine. This was real.

Sally was right, something was wrong.

Ten minutes later Marcus slowly replaced the handset and slumped at his desk, fingers to his temples, for once in his life unable to deal with the enormity of the situation.

Leaning back, he wiped his eyes, shocked to discover them damp. Fumbling a handkerchief out of his pocket with trembling hands, he dabbed at a face suddenly clammy with shock.

As if she'd been waiting for the line busy light to blink off, Sally slipped into the room bearing a cup of fragrantly steaming coffee which she placed before him. Gratefully, he sipped at it, the reviving liquid easing the knot in his throat.

Glancing at his PA, he noticed that same sunlight beaming onto her shining cap of auburn hair and thought how pretty she was, then the notion was trampled by a fresh wave of despair.

"Sally," he began, stopped, cleared his throat.

"I've dismissed the meeting," she swiftly interrupted. "I told them an emergency had arisen which required you to go to New York and that they were to work on what had been discussed so far, and another meeting will be rescheduled on your return." Briefly, she glanced at the notepad that she was never without.

"I've managed to get you a one-way ticket to New York on this evening's flight out of Heathrow at 19:09 hours, and I've alerted the car to collect you from here in an hour."

Swallowing the last gulp of coffee Marcus frowned, her calm efficiency allowing his frenzied thoughts to stop, slow down, and assess.

"An hour?" he enquired. "That's not enough time, I need to go home and pack..."

"No need," retorted Sally. Crossing the office, she opened one of the tall, built-in cupboards and removed an overnight case.

"After that time, you needed to leave for the New York office immediately and had to buy all new clothes and toiletries there, I took the liberty of ensuring a bag of essentials was always here, ready and waiting." She paused, reached into the cupboard again and drew out a suit bag.

"There's also a change of suit for you."

Stunned into silent admiration at her forethought, he finally murmured. "But how...?"

"I liaised with your cleaner and she let me in one day. I packed what I thought was necessary and it's been waiting here ever since."

"Sally, never leave me, I don't know what I'd do without you."

A pleased smile flirted with her copper-painted lips. "I'm just doing my job," she murmured.

The flight was packed. Slumped into a window seat, Marcus turned his face away from the other passengers, going over his mother's phone call again and again, and the horror in her voice.

"Something terrible has happened, oh Marcus, something so terrible..."

"Mother, what is it? What's happened?"

"They weren't supposed to be with him, it was a business trip to see a client upstate..."

"Who was?"

"Walter."

Walter was his sister Monica's stuffed shirt of a husband. Marcus had nothing against him, the man was kind and mild-mannered and adored his wife and child, Marcus just found him incredibly dull.

"What about Walter? Mother, you're not making any sense."

"He was going to see a client, it was late, the police aren't sure, but they think it was a carjacking that went wrong, maybe Walter fought back…"

Marcus frowned, finding that thought unlikely, then focused on his mother's words.

"A carjacking? Mother, what…?"

"He's dead, oh Marcus, he's dead!"

The shock jolted him upright. Walter dead? Okay, he hadn't been Marcus's favourite person, but he'd been nice enough. Furthermore, he was family, his sister's husband…

His brain backtracked to her previous statement. "You said, they shouldn't have been with him … Who, Mother? Who was with him?"

"Your sister and Megan were in the car with him. They shouldn't have been, he should have been alone, but at the last minute, Monica decided they needed some family time, so she booked them into a B&B close to his client … they were going for the weekend. It was going to be a special time for them, and now … now…"

"Are they all right? Mother! Are they all right?"

Renewed weeping echoed down the phone, and Marcus's insides turned liquid with horror.

"Just come, Marcus, please, just come…"

~Chapter Two~
*"your niece hasn't spoken a
word since the incident."*

What felt like an eternity later but was only a matter of a few hours, Marcus entered the hospital room where his weeping mother sat beside his sister's bedside.

Slowly, he crossed the room, his hand gently brushing his mother's hunched shoulders.

He looked at Monica's still face and knew he was too late.

His sister was dead.

"Mother?"

Celeste Blackwood turned, clutched at her son's jacket, and buried her face in its dark, sombre material as she sobbed.

Marcus realised it was the first time he had ever seen his mother cry, the first time she had ever needed him, really needed him.

Pulling the other chair closer, he sat beside her, soothing and gentling, his gaze drawn with unstoppable, horrified fascination to his sister's bruised face.

Marcus was no expert on violence but knew the effects of a fist when he saw them. His sister had been punched, repeatedly and violently, in the face.

Marcus frowned, looking at his mother as she fished a small, lace-edged handkerchief from her bag and dabbed at swollen eyes.

"They beat them and shot them, Marcus. They shot my Monica for a car. She would have given it to them. As for Walter, well, he wouldn't have tried to fight back or do anything stupid..."

Her voice trailed away as if uneasy about maligning, no matter how mildly, a man who would never be able to fight back about anything again.

Marcus's mouth gaped with horror.

You read about such things, saw them on TV, but to have it happen to your own family, to your sister, your brother-in-law, it was beyond belief.

A sudden, awful thought occurred to Marcus.

"What about Megan?"

The doctor led him to a small room in a quiet secluded part of the hospital. It was plush, almost pleasant, and Marcus was thankful his family had money.

Tragedy and death struck with an almost arbitrary will; yet being wealthy undoubtedly eased the blow.

They stopped before entering the room. Marcus peered through the blinded window and saw the small, still form as she lay in the large hospital bed – Megan, his sister's seven-year-old daughter, his niece.

"You're sure she wasn't harmed?"

He turned anxiously towards the doctor, who sighed and shook his head.

"No, physically, Megan's fine. She has contusions on her shoulders where the straps of her car seat chafed when the car abruptly halted.

There's fingertip bruising on her jawline, which indicates her face was grabbed by one of the carjackers, and we have her on a fluid drip as she's refusing to eat or drink. Other than that, physically, she's fine. But..." his voice trailed away.

Marcus turned to face him.

"But?" he prompted.

"But we must remember," continued the doctor. "Whatever happened, Megan was a witness. She saw her parents threatened, beaten, and shot in front of her, before the carjackers left her bound and gagged, lying with her dead father and her critically injured mother by the side of a dark, country road."

"Christ," murmured Marcus, swallowing hard in horror. "How long...?"

"We don't know for sure, certainly overnight. They were on their way to see your brother-in-law's client before going on to a bed and breakfast. When he didn't arrive, the client called the office and his cell phone, but of course the office was closed by then, and as for his cell..."

The doctor's voice trailed away again at the look in Marcus's eyes.

"Anyway," he continued, "his PA found the message the next morning, and she too tried his cell, his home, your sister's cell phone, and the bed and breakfast. When she learnt they never checked in, she became concerned and called the police. They were found early this morning. Your sister was barely alive when she was brought in, but her injuries were too severe; she had lost too much blood."

Marcus braced his hand against the wall and stared through the window, struggling to understand that his sister – his big sister Monica who had bullied and cared for him since he was born – was gone.

That her husband, Walter – a man he had dined with, played golf with – was gone. That their child had experienced such horrors.

Desperately, he tried to focus on the doctor's words.

"So, it's little wonder that Megan is suffering from extreme shock, and I'm very concerned about her. You should know, Mr Blackwood, your niece hasn't spoken a word since the incident. We have tried everything. It's as if she's retreated somewhere deep inside, maybe trying to escape from what's happened."

Marcus looked again at the pale child lying listlessly in the bed.

Rage, white and hot, roared up inside him at the pointless, mindless brutality which had in one stroke ended the worthwhile and productive lives of his sister and her husband, and left their child an orphan, dumb from the horror of her experience.

And for what? A car, a thing.

"Who's that with her?" he asked, noticing the young, pretty woman who sat anxiously by her bedside, one slim hand grasping Megan's unresponsive one in a touch of steadfast support.

"Oh, that's Delphine Pascal, Megan's nanny. She wasn't in the car. I think it was her weekend off. She came as soon as your mother called her and has been here ever since. It's good Megan has someone familiar, someone … calm… with her."

Reading between the lines, Marcus guessed his mother had already been to see her granddaughter and had been unable to control her hysterics.

The woman looked up as he entered and Marcus noted that she was young, early twenties maybe, pretty, and stylish in that unique way that gave away her identity as French before she'd even opened her mouth.

"This is Mr Blackwood," the doctor spoke gently in a low, considerate tone.

"Megan's uncle," he added, as she continued to look blank.

"Oh, yes, of course." Her voice was soft and strongly accented.

Marcus now remembered his mother telling him some time ago of Monica's decision to hire a French nanny, in the hope Megan would pick up a few words of the language.

"Hello, Delphine."

Marcus cast an apprehensive look at Megan's blank countenance.

"How is she?"

Delphine shrugged expressively, the way only Europeans can, then clamped a hand to her mouth as tears swam into her eyes.

Marcus saw the glint of gold on the third finger of her left hand; noted the pretty, little sapphire engagement ring.

"She says nothing; she won't even look at me. It's as if she's not there, not really."

Delphine's English was fragmented, breaking down under pressure.

Automatically, Marcus dropped a hand to her shoulder, squeezing slightly to comfort and reassure. He felt her tense, then relax, under his palm.

"Maybe you could try talking to her," suggested the doctor.

"I don't know…"

Marcus stopped, unwilling to admit his reluctance to go near his catatonic niece, this child who lay there so inert and still, with eyes so wide and staring.

Swallowing down his unease, angry with himself, he eased a chair away from a nearby wall and placed it on the other side of the bed opposite Delphine.

He took Megan's free hand in his, feeling the smallness of her bones in his hand, like bird wings, so delicate and fragile.

For a while, he said nothing.

He was aware of the doctor bustling about behind him, checking the machinery Megan was hooked up to, of Delphine staring over the bed at him, and of Megan's blank eyes gazing at nothing, seeing nothing, responding to nothing.

"Hello, Megan,"

Marcus looked straight at her hoping for something, anything – a flicker, a spark of awareness – but there was nothing.

Was he surprised?

It had been over a year since he had last seen her. Not long to him maybe, but a lifetime ago to Megan.

His eyes fastened on the small, brown, stuffed dog which was lying by her side.

Its fur had been rubbed almost bare in places and one ear was hanging on by a thread, yet Marcus recognised it as the toy he had given her one birthday.

"I'm glad to see you've still got Brewster," he commented, pleased.

"Do you remember the day I gave him to you, Megan?"

Nothing.

No wait, her head turned.

She looked at him, really looked at him, and her hand tightened in his.

Marcus heard Delphine gasp.

Behind him, he felt the doctor become alert with professional interest.

"Talk to her some more," he urged, quietly.

"Do you remember Megan?" Marcus continued, desperately.

"I came to see you and I brought you a present for your birthday, a little brown doggie that needed a home. You didn't know what to call him, so I told you about the dog I'd had when I was a little boy, a little brown doggie called Brewster. We thought it was a good name for a dog, and you decided to call your doggie Brewster, too."

Marcus faltered.

Megan's dark eyes were fixed upon his face with intense concentration.

"Do you remember, Megan?" he asked again, urgently.

Slowly, softly, Megan's small hand released itself from Delphine's grasp, crept across the bedclothes and fastened upon his free hand, drawing it back to rest gently on Brewster's head.

"You do remember, don't you, Megan?" he exclaimed, his voice hoarse with relief and gratitude.

"You do remember me. I'm your Uncle Marcus."

There was a moment, then Megan nodded.
Just once.
But it was enough...

The next day, Marcus stared with dismay at his sister's solicitor with the sinking feeling his life had suddenly become very complicated.

To his disbelief and his mother's consternation, Monica had bequeathed the sole care and upkeep of her only child to him.

At the age of thirty-six, confirmed bachelor, Marcus Blackwood, had become guardian to a seven-year-old girl.

~Chapter Three~
"what Megan needs right now is a home."

The screams rent the night air. Inhuman and bestial, they dragged Marcus from the depths of exhausted slumber, jack-knifing him up in bed, heart pounding as cold, panicky sweat drenched his adrenalin alert body.

Shaking the last fug of sleep from his brain, Marcus rolled out of bed, snatching up his robe from the floor and casting a quick, anxious glance at the clock. 2:05am. He'd had precisely 45 minutes of sleep since the last time.

Quickly, he stuffed his arms into the robe, barely tightening the belt before he was yanking open the bedroom door and rushing down the corridor to where the screams had now subsided into a series of great, gulping, gasping sobs.

It had taken him barely moments to go from solid sleep to battle-ready alertness, yet Delphine was already there before him, crouching on the bed beside the thrashing and shivering child, rocking her, soothing her, murmuring words of comfort in French which she always reverted to in times of stress.

Briefly, the thought flashed through Marcus's mind that he wished Delphine would wear a little more to bed or would take the extra few seconds to at least pull on a robe.

Those skimpy little pink, lace-trimmed bed shorts and a camisole top, although certainly less revealing than a bikini, somehow now, in the dead of night and the confines of his apartment, seemed outrageously erotic.

"How is she?" he enquired, furiously pushing his thoughts away.

Delphine was young enough to be his daughter, well, almost, and was engaged to a handsome, and rugged looking, French botanist to boot. And anyway, whilst she was under his roof taking care of his child, she deserved a little more respect.

Delphine looked up over Megan's blonde head, which was pressing against her neat, pert breasts … Again, Marcus smacked his thoughts down, desperately averting his eyes and feeling an almost schoolboy flush on his cheeks.

Wide-eyed with concern, Delphine let loose a stream of French at him, which had Marcus blinking in incomprehension as she gestured helplessly with her hands.

"She … it is the same as always … those dreams, those … nightmares?"

Marcus nodded at her correct use of the word, and it seemed to calm Delphine, for she took a deep breath and tried again.

"Yes, those nightmares, they will not leave her alone. I think she dreams of what happened, what she saw."

Marcus nodded. That had been his conclusion and it had also been confirmed by the eminent child psychiatrist he was currently taking Megan to three times a week.

Swiftly, he crossed to the bed and tried to prise Megan's vice-like grip from Delphine's arms.

"Megan," he soothed. "Megan, sweetheart, it's okay, it's Uncle Marcus. You're safe, you're home in your bed. You're safe, no one's ever going to hurt you again. Look."

Desperately he picked up the stuffed dog and stroked one soft paw down the child's tear-drenched cheek.

"Here's Brewster, he wants a cuddle."

Megan snatched the dog away and rocked him into her body, her soft, keening wails less frantic now, but still eerily animal-like.

Marcus was reminded of the time he found a rabbit caught in a trap. It had plainly been there some time and its initial panic and pain had settled into an acceptance of the situation. Marcus had knelt beside it, horrified, but feeling an irresistible, ten-year-old boy's fascination.

Gently, he touched its silky soft fur. The rabbit had cast a look at him from somehow knowledgeable eyes, and Marcus understood it knew it was dying. Knew and accepted it.

Marcus wrestled with the trap to free it but in the process, he unwittingly injured the rabbit further. It wailed, a thin, sharp cry which curdled the blood in his veins, and then it had gone still, its eyes dulling over, and Marcus had known it was dead.

Now, as Marcus looked into the eyes of his niece, he saw that same, almost dumb, animal-like acceptance. That pain and suffering were her continual lot. Sudden concern at the long-forgotten, long-buried memory and its frightening parallels gave a sharp edge of panic to his voice.

"Megan," he cried. "Please, stop..."

Maybe she heard.

Maybe she understood.

Or maybe it was being addressed in a tone so different from the soothing, placating voice all adults used around her, but Megan did stop.

She peered at him, blinking through lashes welded together by tears. Beside him, Marcus felt Delphine draw slowly, imperceptibly away as Megan allowed him to pull her into his arms.

As pre-arranged, Delphine crept silently from the room, leaving Marcus to begin the arduous task of calming Megan back to sleep.

When Marcus finally left the room and wearily closed the door on the soundly sleeping child, he found Delphine waiting for him in the lounge.

Blearily, he noted she'd taken the time to pull on a long, enveloping robe and brush her tangled hair, yet knowing what was under the robe was enough to make Marcus blush again and fix his eyes determinedly on her face.

"I made some tea," she said, her accent caressing the word, imbuing it with sensuality. Marcus gratefully accepted the china cup of fragrant liquid served with a madeleine, freshly made by Delphine that afternoon, and sank tiredly into a chair.

"Is she getting any better, Delphine?" he asked in weary resignation, nibbling at the madeleine and noting it was good, very good in fact.

Like most French people, to Delphine food and drink were almost a religion and everything she made, even something as humble as tea and biscuits, seemed to almost absorb that attitude of perfection from her.

"I think so, yes," Delphine nodded seriously. "In the beginning, she was waking six, maybe seven, times a night. Now, it is only four or five, so yes, I think she begins to heal, to accept..."

"But not forget?" Marcus enquired.

"No, she will never forget. But, maybe, with time, the remembering will not be so hard."

"Is there anything else I can do to help her, Delphine?"

"No, no." Delphine was quick to reassure, maybe a little too quick, and Marcus looked at her enquiringly. Under his studied gaze, Delphine became flustered.

"It is just, maybe, this apartment, it does not help..."

"The apartment? What's wrong with it?"

"Nothing, it is a very chic, very smart apartment, but ... it is almost exactly like your sister's, and I think, maybe, that is not so much a good thing."

Marcus frowned, looking around at the spacious, coolly contemporary space, the realisation bursting upon him that Delphine was right. It was exactly like his sister's apartment.

When he had moved in five years ago, his sister had come over to help him decorate and furnish. He had different furniture, and the size and layout of the rooms were different, but in terms of feeling and look and style, the things that would impact on a child and make an impression, it was a carbon copy of the apartment overlooking Central Park where she'd lived for seven years with her parents.

"And you don't think that a sense of familiarity is a good thing in this case?"

"No." Delphine shook her head, dark hair tumbling around her shoulders. "I think some familiarity..."

She stumbled slightly over the difficult word and sighed at her own perceived clumsiness with the English language.

"Some familiarity is good, but being reminded every day of her home, of what she has lost, I do not think that is so good."

"What do you suggest?" Marcus asked concerned, and quickly averted his gaze back up to her face, as Delphine tucked her legs up beneath her, drawing attention to small, shapely feet with shell pink painted toenails.

"Maybe something completely different, more child-friendly, not so ordered, or neat. I think what Megan needs right now is a home."

The next day, after a breakfast throughout which Megan had simply sat, silent as the grave, poking unenthusiastically at her porridge with a spoon with Brewster's paw firmly stuck in her mouth.

Marcus and Delphine chatted brightly, too brightly, about Delphine's plans to take Megan shopping for new clothes and then onto the Victoria & Albert Museum.

Marcus then did what he always did when faced with a situation he couldn't cope with.

He went to see Luke.

Marcus couldn't help but envy his brother his idyllic life. He was now happily settled in a large and sunny modern home in a leafy London suburb, with his wife, Arianna, and her daughter Lucia, after that intensely manic time last year when Luke had first met Arianna.

They had endured a few tense weeks after her first husband, Roberto, had kidnapped Lucia, and Luke had given everything he had to find her and bring her safely home to her mother.

Then there was the horrific hostage situation which had left Roberto dead and Arianna seriously wounded.

Marcus was happy for his brother, of course, he was, but... he also envied him a little.

"Hi, Uncle Marcus."

Marcus blinked away his thoughts as the door was opened by Lucia, beaming all over her face and as pretty as a picture in a pink, ruffled sundress.

"Hey, midget," he retorted. "No school today?"

"Duh." Lucia rolled her eyes at his stupidity as only a nine-year-old could. "It's the school holidays."

"Is it?" Marcus paused, reflecting how he would have to start paying attention to things like that now. Although, the notion of Megan ever being well enough to return to school seemed impossible; a far-away fantasy destined never to come true.

"Okay, cool. Mum and Dad around?"

"Mum!"

Letting out a bellow to summon home the cows, Lucia skipped away into the cool interior, leaving Marcus to shut the front door and follow, noticing the freshly hung artwork on the walls.

It had taken Arianna a long time to recover from being shot by Roberto, and they had only finally moved into their dream home a couple of months ago. Each time Marcus visited there were new things to see and admire.

"Hey, Marcus."

Arianna appeared at the kitchen door, her slim form wrapped in a flour splotched apron, a caked wooden spoon in hand, and a smear of flour on her glowing cheek.

"Hey, gorgeous."

Marcus carefully kissed the other cheek. Mindful of his charcoal suit, he avoided the flour.

Smelling her subtle fragrance and feeling the whisper of chestnut curls against his face, he thought again how lucky his brother was.

"Luke about?"

"In the garden." Arianna paused, studying his expression. "Is everything ok? How's Megan?"

Marcus shrugged, unwilling to admit there was no change and that his niece still hadn't uttered a single word to anyone.

"Delphine thinks there's some improvement. She's waking less in the night. Maybe she's beginning to accept the situation."

Arianna slowly nodded, her eyes never leaving his face. Surprising them both, she threw her arms about him and gave him a fierce hug.

Stunned, Marcus returned it, uncaring of the flour and his suit, not even minding when the cookie dough wooden spoon tapped him on the shoulder, drawing strength from her soft, womanly concern, and wishing...

Wishing he had *this* in his life.

"Stay for lunch," she offered.

At his doubtful expression, she shook his arm.

"Stay for lunch," she insisted, then laughed and drew him into the kitchen.

Releasing him, she passed him an open bottle of wine and a pair of oversized glasses.

"Here," she ordered. "Take these, go and talk to Luke, lunch will be about an hour."

He took the offerings and smiled in thanks, chuckling as she made shooing motions towards the open, full-width glass doors.

~Chapter Four~
"It must have a treehouse."

Pausing to remove his jacket, Marcus shook his head ruefully at the flour stains, then hung it over the back of a kitchen chair and wandered out onto the decking.

Shading his eyes, he looked around the pleasant oasis of a garden, finally spotting Luke in the far corner.

He was pacing around and looking up into the branches of a huge, wide-spreading oak tree. He appeared to be arguing with himself, or maybe it was with the tree.

Marcus cocked a brow as he approached and caught his brother's attention, warmed by the immediate, welcoming smile that beamed across Luke's face.

"Hey there," exclaimed Luke, then spotted the wine and glasses. "Oh, liking the look of that."

"Arianna gave them to me. She told me lunch will be an hour, and that I am staying for it."

Luke chuckled, took a glass, and nodded appreciatively as Marcus filled it. He then gestured to a charming wrought iron table and chairs set in the welcome shade beneath the tree.

Marcus filled the other glass, placed the bottle on the table, and settled himself into the other chair, glad of shelter from the fierce, mid-morning sun. He glanced up at the sturdy boughs above.

"Has the tree offended you?" he remarked.

"What?" Swallowing his wine, Luke followed his gaze in confusion, then his expression cleared, and he laughed. "No, I was trying to see if it would be possible to build a treehouse up there, for Lucia."

"A treehouse?"

"Yeah, remember that great one we used to have?"

Marcus smiled, recalling with a pang, those long-ago childhood days, when he and Luke, both back from their respective boarding schools, would practically spend the whole of those everlasting summer holidays in the branches of a giant copper beech, in what he fondly remembered as being the best treehouse in the world.

"I remember," he mused, taking a sip of wine. "That was a *really* great treehouse."

"The best," agreed Luke. "Do you remember when Susannah got old enough to walk? All she wanted was to come into the treehouse with us?"

"I remember we used to pull the ladder up behind us and laugh while she cried below. We were mean little sods back then," Marcus chuckled.

"Yeah, soon changed though when she began to bring her pretty schoolfriends home. We couldn't get that ladder down quick enough then." Luke paused and glanced at Marcus.

"So, how are things?"

"Okay," Marcus began automatically, then shook his head. "Not so good," he admitted.

"Megan's sleeping a bit better, only screaming the house down five or six times a night instead of the seven or eight it was in the beginning."

"Still not talking?"

"No, not a single word since... well, since it happened."

"Poor little mite," agreed Luke, his kindly face creasing in sympathy.

"Yeah, Delphine's been amazing. But it's only another month and then she's off back to France."

"You can't persuade her to stay a little longer?"

"No, they've already postponed the wedding once. I can't ask them to do it again."

Luke nodded in understanding, and harmony descended as the two men sipped in synchronised silence, smiling at each other as a strain of a song warbled by Lucia floated out to them from the house.

"So, how's Marla?"

"Delphine says Megan needs a home."

They stopped, each waited for the other to continue, smirked, sipped wine again. Marcus waved at Luke indicating he should speak first.

"I was wondering," Luke began again. "How's Marla?"

Marcus considered the question. How was Marla? Thinking about his on/off girlfriend was always guaranteed to make him squirm. A model, hungrily pursuing catwalk fame, she was beautiful, sharp, intelligent, and selfish.

Aware it was purely a physical thing, Marcus was amazed it had lasted as long as it had, but then he was rich, secure in his world, and not unpleasant to look at.

They made a handsome couple, one the celebrity mags loved. And it had been fun, being seen with her, having a backstage pass to the glamorous world she inhabited.

Then he became an instant father to a traumatised, silent, seven-year-old, and everything changed. No longer able to constantly squire her about town as an on-tap plus one, Marcus had sensed her interest in him waning.

Desperately, he had introduced her to Megan, and to give her credit, Marla had tried – in her own way. Bringing a selection of beauty products, she had tried to interest Megan in a girlie make-up session, even going so far as to plaster paint and powder on Megan's unresponsive face.

Delphine had been out for the evening, and Marcus had been in the kitchen putting together a "family" meal for them.

Coming back into the room, he'd been disturbed to find Megan looking like a clown, sitting on the edge of the coffee table, and staring unremittingly at Marla who was gabbling away about a photoshoot in Milan she had just returned from.

Perhaps he had been a little sharper with Marla than he should have been. After all, a make-over by a proper model would have thrilled any other little girl. But Megan wasn't like any other little girl, and to see her tiny, innocent face covered with make-up, well, something inside him had snapped.

He asked Marla to leave, rather curtly and had gently cleaned all the paint off Megan's face, cuddling her and Brewster close to his chest until she fell asleep, and he could carefully put her to bed.

Now, at Luke's question, he shrugged, indicating it was a subject he did not wish to discuss. Understanding, in the shorthand way the brothers had, Luke changed the subject.

"A home? But hasn't she already got a home?"

"Yes, but..."

Marcus paused, gathering his thoughts.

"Delphine feels it's too much like her old home in New York, and that it's reminding her too much of ... well, her mum and her dad."

Luke nodded, his expression sobering at the thought of his older half-sister's brutal demise.

"Have the police any leads at all? About what happened, or who could have done this?"

"No. If Megan could talk, could tell them anything, maybe a description of the man who murdered her parents ... but she won't, can't, not yet anyway."

"It *was* random, wasn't it?" At the sharp note in Luke's voice, Marcus lifted a brow in enquiry.

"I mean, I wouldn't imagine Monica had any enemies, but what about Walter? Wasn't he a big shot in corporate finance?"

Marcus paused, Luke's questions triggering a thought, a memory, which had been buried so deep it was only now surfacing.

"He called me," he began, slowly.

"Who?"

"Walter. He called me a few days before it happened. He sounded worried, said he wanted to talk to me."

"What about?"

"I'm not sure, he didn't say, not exactly. The whole conversation was a bit bizarre, now I come to think of it. He called me at work and asked if he could tell me something strictly confidential that I wasn't to talk to anyone about. I said, of course, but to be honest, I wasn't listening because ... well ... because it was Walter, and you know what he was like."

He paused, gestured helplessly, and Luke nodded. Yes, he did indeed know what Walter was like. Having only met him a couple of times at family functions, Luke had formed an impression of a fussy, pedantic man.

What his control freak of a sister saw in him was anyone's guess, but perhaps a man who never answered back was her idea of a perfect mate.

Feeling mean for having such thoughts, Luke asked, "Did you ever find out what he wanted?"

"Well, not exactly. He began to talk about what to do when you suspected someone had broken your trust. But he took so long to get to this point, that I'd begun reading a report about oil prices in the Middle East. Then he said he needed proof before he could act. I asked him 'act on what', and he went all cagey and changed the subject as if someone else had walked into the room."

"Monica?"

"No, I don't think so, he was phoning from his office so one of his colleagues maybe. As I said, the whole thing was very strange."

"And a few days later, he was dead," commented Luke, mildly.

"Yes," agreed Marcus slowly. "A few days later, he was dead." He looked sharply at Luke.

"You don't think...?"

Luke shrugged.

"It's probably nothing but it is coincidental, and I've never believed in coincidences. Still, I don't suppose there's anything we can do about it now, leastways not unless Megan starts talking and can remember what happened that night."

"Do you think finding her a home would help?"

"What do you think?"

"Maybe I could look around, find somewhere, sell the apartment."

"Do you want to? After all, it's been your home for five years."

Marcus considered the question. "It's where I live," he finally said. "I've no attachment to it."

Luke looked as if he wanted to say more and looking up into the leafy boughs, Marcus hastily changed the subject.

"A treehouse huh? Cool. Does Lucia know about it yet?"

That night, in between Megan's outbursts, Marcus dreamt about their old treehouse and the fun they used to have in it.

Before dawn, he slipped into another dream memory, of the day his father had told him he and Marina, his stepmother, were divorcing.

Shifting uneasily in his bed, Marcus remembered lying in the treehouse crying inconsolably, Luke distraught and trying to comfort him, both assuming that Marcus would be taken away by his father.

Then the relief he felt upon discovering he was to stay with Marina, Luke, and Susannah, his care to be included in his father's maintenance payments for his half-siblings.

Both his father and Marina openly acknowledging George Blackwood's inability to give a child the loving home he needed.

Sitting bolt upright in bed, Marcus realised he knew exactly what he had to do.

Next morning, giving Sally a list of calls to make, appointments to arrange and other business-related affairs, Marcus paused, and Sally arched her perfectly shaped brows at him.

"Anything else?" she enquired.

"Yes, Sally, I want you to find me a house."

"A house?"

"Yes, a house."

"You mean, you want to move to a different apartment?"

"No, I mean I want a house, a home. Somewhere cosy, with character, and with doors that height charts can be measured on. One with a kitchen that's the heart of the home, and a garden, it must have a big, rambling garden."

"I see."

Sally was busy jotting down all his requirements, not by a flicker showing even a degree of surprise at his sudden and bizarre request.

"I'll get right on it."

"Thank you, oh, and Sally…"

"Yes?"

"It must have a treehouse."

~Chapter Five~
"We can't afford to live here anymore."

Five-thirty and the early evening sun was still beating down with radioactive force. Marcus shifted uncomfortably on the doorstep, his skin prickling between his shoulder blades and sweat oozing under his dark suit.

Impatiently, he rang the bell again.

For heaven's sake, where was the woman? The appointment was for five-thirty, and he didn't have time to hang around. Delphine was with Megan, but he still liked to be there at bedtime.

He had made the decision not to drag Megan along with him for the first round of house hunting. Thinking back to the three viewings he had already done, that was a wise decision.

There had been nothing wrong with the houses he had seen that day; Sally had done her job admirably. But each one had had a flaw, a fault, something to pick at and cause him to reject them instantly.

House number one was too far out of the city centre; thinking about the commute in rush hour traffic was enough to make him shudder. House two had had a treehouse, true, but a round, silver, alien pod-like contraption reached by a rope ladder wasn't exactly what he had in mind. House number three had been wrong. No logical explanation, just wrong.

So here he was, standing on the doorstep of house number four, his final viewing for the day. Hot, tired, hungry, thirsty, and beginning to get a little pissed off, he glanced impatiently around the front of the property, thinking the owners had no idea of the importance of curb appeal when selling your home.

Old, broken pots lurched crazily on either side of the door, all sporting an impressive display of cracked dirt. Looking up, he saw antique cobwebs draped in the corners of the porch and shuddered at the thought of their desiccated corpse contents falling on him.

The door itself, although flanked by rather beautiful panels of stained glass, was in desperate need of a fresh coat of paint, its brass furnishings tarnished and grubby.

Finally, he saw movement through the glass, an arm lifted, and the door was flung open.

"I'm so sorry," she gasped. "I was fetching the washing in and didn't realise how late it was. Please, come in, you must be boiled alive standing there."

Marcus blinked, taken aback, then recovered himself and held out a slightly clammy hand.

"I'm Marcus Blackwood," he said. "I believe you spoke with my PA?"

"Yes, lovely lady. Oh, yes." She held out a slim, suntanned hand with nails short almost to the quick, and clasped his in a firm handshake. "I'm Grace Lovejoy. Please, won't you come in?"

Relieved to be out of the fierce afternoon sun, Marcus stepped into the cool, shady interior, glancing around with interest as she closed the front door. Stepping by him in a swirl of tie-dyed skirt and a hint of patchouli, she gestured vaguely around the space.

"This is the front hall, obviously. Sorry, it's a bit of a mess." With a frown and a tut, she swept a pile of school cardigans and bags from the bottom of the stairs, looked helplessly around, then dumped them with a sigh of resignation onto a nearby chair which was pushed back at a crazy angle against a wall.

"It's lovely," said Marcus, looking underneath the clutter and dust to see the stunning, chequered, black and white floor tiles, the grand sweep of the staircase, and the brass stair rods visible even under the grime.

Doors opened off in all directions and his gaze flicked up to the high ceiling, the ornate cornicing, the original panelled doors, and white china door furnishings.

A flicker of something. Interest? Excitement? Anticipation? Jumped in his gut. Yet he remained silent, poker face in place, waiting for her next move and silently studying her.

She was tiny, five-foot at most, and slender to the point of skinny. Under the straps of her khaki vest top, he could see shoulder blades jutting. A tangle of beaded necklaces and pendants on thongs around her neck matched the cacophony of bangles on each wrist and the long, knotted leather belt that hung ineffectively around her hips.

The tie-dyed skirt he noticed before was purple, with varying swirls of bleached patterns dancing crazily over the fabric. Reaching almost to her ankles, it stopped short of the gold ankle bracelet which tinkled every time she moved, courtesy of the tiny bells attached to it.

Hippie, he thought dismissively, considering the unmade up, tanned face, and noting the small nose piercing and the dreadlocked hair.

What a pompous, arrogant stuffed shirt thought Grace, keeping her best company smile firmly fixed on her face. Look at him, eyeing her up, judging, labelling, finding her wanting.

Oh, she had met his type before. Still, he was rich, with a wallet that could afford the exorbitant price tag the estate agents had slapped on the house.

And handsome.

Even she was forced to admit that.

Very handsome. Classically so. Tall, dark, square-jawed, and those piercing blue eyes. Shame those looks were wasted on someone with all the personality of a brick.

"Shall I show you around?" she asked, her heart sinking as it did, each time she had to put her nest on show, offering it up for inspection.

Watching the lips curl as she showed them room after room, each one needing extensive renovation, each one a pile of children's clutter and the detritus of a busy life she never quite had the time to tidy up.

This is my home, she wanted to scream. Can't you see that it's killing me to have to move? Do you think I want to sell it? Want to see it go to the likes of someone like you? Someone who can't love it the way we do. Could never feel about this place the way we do. But she always remained silent, obliging, showing them everything they wanted to see, and gritting her teeth at their perceived, silent condemnation.

Unsurprised after they had left – thanking her, promising to think about it – to get the estate agents call the next day telling her it hadn't quite been what they'd been looking for.

"Plebs," she dismissed them every time. "Didn't want them to get it anyway."

But the truth was the situation was getting desperate. Her savings were almost all gone, sucked into the black hole that was the house. It consumed money like an ever-hungry mouth. The huge energy bills, despite them wearing three layers in the winter to avoid putting the heating on. The massive council tax bill. Endless niggly repairs that mounted up in desperate necessity and cost.

Finally, three months ago, she called a family meeting, sat the kids down in the kitchen and laid all her cards on the table. She told them the truth and spelt out the inevitable future if they continued the way they were.

The boys had been silent, stunned by her brutality, unable to understand. Too young to grasp mundane, boring adult concepts such as tax, insurances, and mortgages.

Zoey understood though. Perched on a chair, her long, messy plait touched the scarred wood of the table as she bent forward in thought.

"There's nothing else for it then, Mum," she announced, looking at Grace with those old-soul eyes of hers. "We have to sell the house, move into something smaller and cheaper to run."

"What?" howled the twins. "We can't leave here, we can't..."

"Be quiet," snapped Zoey. As usual, her voice had more sway over them than Grace's ever did.

"We can't afford to live here anymore. That's the truth so now we deal with it. Don't worry, Mum," she turned to Grace, gripping her hand. "It'll be okay, you'll see, something will turn up."

Looking into her daughter's earnest, fifteen-year-old face, Grace reflected not for the first time how getting accidentally pregnant at sixteen was the best thing that could ever have happened to her because it brought Zoey into the world.

A child who was meant to be born. Was meant to be here. Was an ever-constant source of strength and joy in Grace's hard life.

So now, for Zoey's sake, for the sake of Finley and Connor, she fixed on her most polite smile and gestured to the stairs.

"Shall we start at the top and work our way down?"

Good grief, thought Marcus, in disbelief. Didn't this woman want to sell her house? Not everyone was a born salesman, but everyone should know how to make a basic effort.

Surely, it should be common sense to anyone that it wasn't a clever idea to do nothing but point out the faults – the leaking tap in the bathroom, the limescale in the bath, the ill-fitting windows that plainly all needed replacing, the centuries-old boiler, the dodgy looking patch of damp on a bedroom ceiling. Why was she drawing his attention to these?

Why wasn't she emphasising its good points, showing him the best features of this lovely old house?

Because it *was* lovely.

Following her around from room to room, Marcus's keen eye took note of the gorgeous lofty ceilings, the fireplaces in every room, the ornate skirting boards and door lintels, and the little squares of stained glass over each bedroom door.

Finally, she led him up a steep flight of stairs to a cluttered and dusty, but surprisingly spacious, set of rooms under the eaves.

Carefully avoiding his suit on the cobwebs, Marcus wandered over to the window and peered through its grimy panes, noting the large and overgrown garden below, and wondering, with a clutch of interest, which tree had the house in it.

The woman was speaking again, and out of politeness, he tuned back into her voice.

"I always planned to turn this space into a master suite," she was saying, "but there was never enough money."

Intrigued, Marcus looked around, gingerly picked his way across the cluttered floor, and opened doors, peering into the other rooms.

She was right; it cried out to be a master suite. Thinking, he looked about. Yes, there was certainly enough room.

Large bedroom this side with a balcony overlooking the garden, then a walk-in wardrobe and bathroom the other end. There might even be enough room for a small study.

"Yes," he agreed, nodding. "That would be an excellent use of the space."

The woman blinked at him, and Marcus realised it was the first time he had spoken to her since the hall.

Gathering his manners, he treated her to the full wattage of a Blackwood boy smile.

Looking a little dazed, she gestured back towards the stairs.

"Shall we go down, look at the ground floor and the garden?"

"Yes, please, by all means," he agreed politely, his heart doing a weird little jump at the word garden.

Following her down the stairs, he thought once again how special a house this could be with some care and attention.

And money. A lot of money, he added wryly. It could be amazing.

But it was a big house, too big for him and Megan. Even with the nanny, he had to hire to replace Delphine, it was still a lot of house for three people.

It needed a family.

More than that, it needed a large family to fill its rooms with life and laughter.

He tried to imagine living here with Megan.

He tried to imagine living here with Marla and smiled in disbelief.

~Chapter Six~
"It's our house; he's not getting it,"

Downstairs, there were four generous reception rooms. But it was plain by the abandoned, dusty state of them, that the family mostly lived in the huge kitchen that stretched across the back of the house, opening onto a green, shady garden that enticed and beckoned alluringly through a part-glazed back door.

Get rid of that, thought Marcus, then open-up the entire back wall with those amazing folding doors he had seen at Luke and Arianna's. The kitchen was massive but cluttered and dirty. Seriously, would it kill the woman to clean once in a while?

Walking in, he found a tall, red-haired girl standing at the stove stirring something that bubbled in a large pot with one hand, an open book held in the other.

She turned at their entrance. Marcus judged her to be in her mid-teens, but there was a sober seriousness to her gaze; a wisdom in her eyes that spoke of an age far beyond her years.

"This is my daughter, Zoey," the woman said, and Marcus inclined his head politely.

"Hello, Zoey."

"This is Mr Blackwood," she continued, to her daughter. "He's here to look at the house," she added, unnecessarily.

Zoey nodded, looked him up and down, then returned to her cooking, putting down her book to season whatever it was that smelt so good.

"Where are your brothers?" asked her mother.

Zoey shrugged and replied without turning.

"In the treehouse."

Again, Marcus felt that clutch of anticipation. This was ridiculous. Why now? Why, after all these years, was he having these memories? Was it because of Megan? Had her fear and helplessness somehow triggered recollections of a time in his life when he too had felt adrift and confused, alone and scared?

Following the woman out into the garden, he blinked in the strong, slanting evening sunlight that dappled the grass through the trees. Looking around, he took in the large garden which meandered away around corners with overgrown paths beckoning you to explore.

It was an amazing garden, or rather, he amended, it could be. Once again, neglect and lack of care were all too evident in the long grass, the overgrown beds, the scarred and battered garden furniture, and the towering trees in desperate need of a trim.

A portly, black and white husky lay panting in the shade, not bothering to get up as they walked by him. "Hey, Badger," murmured the woman.

The dog lifted its head in acknowledgement, opening vivid blue eyes behind its robber-like black and white face markings, then flopped down again as if the effort had been too much.

"Where's the treehouse?" Unable to contain himself any longer, he had to ask.

The woman startled at his abruptness and then smiled, her whole face lighting up into natural beauty. "It's through here," she replied.

She led the way down one of those enticing paths to where the garden surprisingly opened back up again into a large and well-stocked vegetable plot.

Where the rest of the garden was neglected and overgrown, here everything was tidy and precision neat. Long rows of healthy plants burgeoning with edible life, edged up to a chicken coop in which plump hens fussily clucked and scratched at the soil, watched over by a magnificent cockerel.

"You have chickens," he exclaimed, hooking his fingers through the wire fence, and gazing in fascination. A city boy, he'd never seen chickens before unless they were oven-ready in Harrods food hall, and he tried to imagine Megan's reaction to these motherly-looking birds.

"Yes," the woman confirmed. "Although, they'll be going with us," she hastily reassured.

Intrigued, Marcus gazed around the vegetable patch. "Your vegetables look healthy," he said, unwilling to admit he was unable to identify any of them, except, wait ... "The carrots in particular," he added, spotting tell-tale orange caps crowning through the rich, dark soil.

"I know," agreed the woman, proudly. "I have an allotment as well. We never have to buy vegetables. I grow enough to feed us the entire year through. And fruit," she added, gesturing to where he could see soft fruit bushes, now empty of their seasonal load.

Further along, a large apple tree was bowed down with its russet harvest. A few had dropped to the ground, and wasps, drunk on cider, crawled busily over the spoilt fruit. Further still, right in the bottom corner of the garden, Marcus saw an impressive compost heap and standing off to one side of it what looked like two, upturned, Ali Baba laundry baskets.

Small black dots were busily humming around it, enabling Marcus to make an educated guess as to what they were. "You have bees?"

"Yes," the woman replied. "Well, they're my daughter, Zoey's. They're her passion. None of the rest of us is allowed anywhere near her hives. But they do make the most wonderful honey."

Seeing the apprehension on his face, she hurriedly added. "Don't worry, they'll be going with us as well."

"How do you move beehives?"

"Carefully," came the drawled reply and Marcus felt his lips twitch in response. "Finley, Connor!" The woman shattered the peaceful idyll of the garden with a bellow, making Marcus jump. "You let down this ladder immediately. The gentleman wants to look at the treehouse."

Looking up, Marcus saw another enormous apple tree. Its branches wide and encompassing, it filled the entire corner of the garden, and there, safely perched in its boughs, was the treehouse.

It was perfect. Sturdy and wooden, it was a proper house with a window. It had plainly been there some time; the wood having mellowed in colour to almost match the trunk of the tree.

It blended so perfectly behind the rustling leaves, that without the woman's pointing finger and accusing glare, Marcus might not have seen it. He edged closer, fascinated, wondering how to get into it, then saw a small balcony at the back of the house, a wooden ladder pulled up from the ground resting on its solid planks.

The woman planted her hands on her hips and scowled into the branches. "Boys," she demanded. "Let down this ladder immediately."

"Shan't," came the cheeky answer. "It's our house; he's not getting it. We're not going."

Looking up, Marcus saw a pair of dark heads bob up over the edge of the windowsill, then quickly disappear back down from view again.

"You are in so much trouble, you two," threatened their mother. "Ladder! Now!"

"Won't!"

A second later, a rotten tomato sailed through the air to explode like a scarlet bomb against the lapel of Marcus's favourite Ralph Lauren suit.

Time stood still. Grace clamped both hands to her mouth in horror staring in mortification at the damage to his suit. Oh, my word, his suit! His suit! A suit that probably cost more than her grocery bill for six months, no, make that a year.

With a face like chiselled granite, he looked down and picked off the squished tomato, staring at it as if he'd never seen a fresh tomato before in his life, he dropped it to the ground.

Looking down at the damage, he seemed bewildered, as if not knowing what to say or do next. Staggering forward, Grace held out a hand in appeasement.

"I am so, so, so sorry," she gasped. "Boys!" She yelled over her shoulder in *that* voice. The one they knew not to disobey, not if they wanted to live to see their eleventh birthdays.

Sheepishly, a pair of heads appeared at the window. With a sharp downward gesture of her index finger and a look – a look they also knew meant big trouble – she indicated they'd better get down here now, on the double.

Exchanging glances, they hung their heads. Knowing they had gone too far this time; they lifted the ladder from the balcony and let it down until it touched the ground.

Looking back at Marcus, she could have sworn she saw his mouth twitch, yet he remained silent.

"I am so sorry," she said again. "Please, let me try and clean that for you." Pulling a not too clean, scrunched up tissue from the pocket of her skirt, she moved towards him.

Marcus reeled back, hands up to ward off the crazy lady. "No, no." He spoke at last. "It's fine, honestly, don't worry. I'll take it to my dry cleaners, they're very good, I'm sure they'll be able to …" he paused, looked afresh at the slaughter on his suit, again his lips twitched. "get the stains out, really, don't worry."

By now the boys had climbed down. Feet dragging, heads bowed almost to their knees in identical misery, they edged over to Grace.

She glared at them, resisting the urge to clout them around the ears. Grace had never lifted a finger to her children, but there were times, oh lord, were there times…

"What do you say?" she demanded.

"Sorry," they drawled, in united misery.

Grace cupped a hand to her ear. "I must be getting deaf in my old age," she scoffed. "Call that an apology?"

"We're sorry for throwing a tomato at you and hitting you," they expanded. Then Finley, or it might have been Connor, added, "Though we weren't aiming for you, we were aiming at mum."

"Then we should all be relieved your aim isn't up to much." Marcus finally spoke.

Grace looked at him to see his eyes twinkling with suppressed merriment, his lips now held so firmly together she could visibly see his ongoing struggle not to laugh.

"We didn't mean it," confirmed Connor or possibly Finley, earnestly. "And we'll pay for the suit if you can't get the stain out. We have money in our box."

"Pay for it?" laughed Grace. "Do you two have any idea how much a suit like this costs?"

The guilty pair shook heads, looking at Marcus. "How much would it be?" Connor asked, his face screwed up in angst. "Cos if it's more than £10, we might have to owe it to you."

"How much to replace the suit?" asked Marcus, and Grace caught a ghost of a wink sent in her direction. "Oh, about a million pounds."

The boys' eyes widened. Helplessly they glanced at one another.

"Told you it was a stupid idea," Finley muttered, only to be punched by his twin.

"Did not," insisted Connor.

"Boys, stop that," insisted Grace, seeing this could escalate fast. "Now, go and get washed for dinner and help your sister lay the table."

"Yes, Mum," they drawled and trailed away, worry evident in every line of their repentant bodies. Helplessly, Grace looked at Marcus.

"I am sorry," she said again. "I don't know what got into them. I know they're upset about having to move, having to leave their home, but that's still no excuse."

"Why are you selling? If you don't mind me asking?" Marcus looked around the little slice of boyhood paradise, glanced up at the treehouse, itching to explore it himself. "You all seem so settled and happy here, why are you leaving?"

"I can't afford it anymore," she replied, simply. "I don't want to move, none of us does, but it's so expensive to run this place. It needs repairs and my savings are all gone." She shrugged away the pain, her arms wrapped around her chest, but he felt it. "We have to sell, get somewhere smaller, cheaper to run and easier to look after." Her voice shook. He heard the raw angst behind them and her honesty shocked yet touched him.

This woman, young despite the age of her daughter, pretty in her own way, standing before him and confessing her inability to pay for her home suddenly became real to him. Not just someone trying to sell him a house, but a real, thinking, feeling person.

"I'm sorry," he murmured, feeling the inadequacy of his words.

She shrugged away his apology. "It is, what it is," she said and smiled. A weary, resigned smile, it nonetheless lit up her face, and Marcus saw through the tired lines and pierced nose to the woman underneath. A woman at the end of the line. A woman who had tried everything to keep her home, but in the end had failed.

"I think I should go," he said.

Grace smiled. He saw the resignation in her eyes. The knowledge that although she might sell her home at some point, it would not be to him.

~Chapter Seven~
"Grace Lovejoy, that was her name."

"I have a call for you on line two." Sally's voice over the intercom startled him from his daydream in which he and Megan lived quite happily in a treehouse, deep in an enchanted wood, and she was talking, really talking, to him.

"A call?" Hearing the sleepiness in his voice he tried to pull himself together. This drifting away during working hours had to stop.

"Yes, it's Maxwell Miles," Sally paused as if that were enough.

"Maxwell, sorry, who?"

"He was deputy CEO under your brother-in-law, Walter. You met him once, at that charity gala his company held last year."

"Oh, yes, him, okay, thanks, Sally, put him through."

Wondering why Maxwell Miles, of all people, was calling him, Marcus picked up the handset.

"Hello?"

"Good morning, Marcus. Or is it afternoon there? I never can quite get the hang of time differences."

As the man's oily, New York accented voice oozed from the handset, Marcus remembered him in an instant.

He also remembered that he hadn't liked him, recalling the man's sycophantic manner, his combed over thinning hair and habit of rubbing his hands together whilst talking to you.

Thinking about the sound of his dry palms rasping together was enough to make Marcus's skin crawl with distaste.

"Good morning, Mr Miles. What can I do for you? I trust you are well?"

"Oh, yes, adequate, you know. Of course, the company is struggling to come to terms with the loss of Walter, such a truly great man."

Gritting his teeth – after all, the man was only saying pleasant things, so why did it feel like the opposite – Marcus forced himself to relax.

"Yes, the death of my sister and Walter was a great shock to us all."

"Indeed, senseless, totally senseless, and that is precisely why I'm calling. To offer my condolences, personally, for your loss."

"Thank you," replied Marcus, wondering what it was about this man that set the hackles on the back of his neck rising, his stomach roiling, and every nerve ending recoiling in distrust.

"And I was wondering if I might enquire as to the well-being of little Megan? Has she recovered at all from the awful events of that simply shocking night?"

"Physically, she's well," Marcus answered slowly. "But unfortunately, she still hasn't regained her voice, hasn't said anything since the… incident. The experts seem to all agree it's from the shock."

"Of course, of course," oozed the voice down the phone. "Poor little girl. Such a bright child as well. I remember she would come into the office, so bright, so observant, such a chatty, talkative child, always commenting on what she'd seen and who she'd met, lovely child, quite lovely."

Compliments again, so why did they make Marcus want to rip the man's windpipe out and beat him with it?

"Yes," he reluctantly agreed, fighting the urge to slam the phone down. "But we're hopeful she will recover in time and will be able to talk again."

"Really? That is excellent news. Well, I must be going, multi-national global corporations don't run themselves, you know," he chuckled.

Marcus remained silent.

"So glad Megan is improving. Please pass on my condolences to the rest of your family, and I would be much obliged if you could keep me updated as to little Megan's condition so I can tell the rest of the staff. She was much loved, you know, and everyone here is rooting for her."

"Of course," Marcus murmured. "Thank you. Now, I am sorry, but I must…"

"Absolutely, busy men, us captains of industry. Thank you for talking to me. Good day." After he had hung up, Marcus sat thinking for a moment, then buzzed through to Sally.

"Yes?"

"If Maxwell Miles calls again, I'm in a meeting. I'm *always* in a meeting."

"Understood."

That weekend Delphine was away in France for a few days, busy with last-minute arrangements for her wedding. Only two more weeks and then she would be gone for good.

Marcus closed his mind to the thought, and to the fact he had done nothing to replace her, then felt angry with himself. This ostrich-like burying his head in the sand was new to him and he didn't like it. Didn't like it one bit. Usually, he was decisive, in charge, organised.

But then this situation was completely alien to him, so maybe he could forgive himself for feeling overwhelmed and unable to cope.

They had been invited to Saturday lunch by Luke and Arianna, so he helped Megan get into her prettiest dress. Sitting on the bed in front of her he gently brushed her hair and tied it up in bunches, his large fingers fumbling with unfamiliar ribbons.

Turning her to see herself in the mirror, he looked at their reflection over her shining head.

"You look very pretty, Megan. I like this dress you and Delphine bought. Do you like it?" He waited for a beat for her to answer. She didn't. He ploughed on regardless. "I hope you have a good time today, Megan. I know Lucia's looking forward to seeing you again."

Silence. Looking at her shuttered eyes, Marcus felt a wave of helplessness pass over him.

"Megan, honey, please say something, anything, it could be anything, but please, please, talk to me."

She stared at him in the mirror. For a moment he dared to hope, felt convinced she was about to talk. Her lips parted as if words hovered on the tip of her tongue … then the instant passed, and her mouth closed.

Disappointment smote him, but then she turned to look at him, looked straight at him, and one small hand came up to touch his cheek.

Holding his breath, Marcus put his hand over hers and they stayed that way for long seconds, frozen in time – him sitting on the bed in front of her, their hands joined on his face. Then she took that tiny step forward, put her arms around him, and hugged him.

Breathing out a relieved gasp, Marcus held her, gently at first then tighter, feeling her little girl body pressed trustingly to his. A vast, rolling wave of protective love, drenched him from head to foot, and he realised how much he had come to love his small niece over the past months.

No, his daughter, she was his daughter now. Even though he had a piece of paper from a judge in New York stating he had become her father many weeks ago, it was only now he realised it was the truth.

Lunch was pleasant, Marcus immensely enjoyed being in his brother and sister-in-law's undemanding, and uncomplicated, company. Relaxing for the first time in weeks, and encouraged by that morning's moment with Megan, he was hopeful that soon, very soon, Megan would talk to him.

Lucia, plainly primed by her mother, was being especially kind and gentle to Megan who sat stiffly in her chair at the table, Brewster clutched in her lap as normal.

Now and then, Marcus would feel her eyes watching him, and he would smile and wink at her. He was rewarded with seeing her unclench a little, and even eat a tiny amount of the delicious Italian food in front of her.

"So," he leant back, happily full of tiramisu and smiling at Luke and Arianna. "When are you guys off on holiday?"

"Next week," confirmed Luke, as Arianna rose and began to clear the table. "Yep, three weeks in the Caribbean, here we come."

"Daddy's going to teach me how to windsurf," chipped in Lucia eagerly.

"Hey, Midget, that's awesome," Marcus smiled at her excitement. "Just beware of the sharks."

"There are no sharks where we're going," Lucia scoffed, then her confidence wavered, and she glanced at Luke. "Daddy?"

"Ignore your Uncle Marcus, he's teasing you." Luke waved away her concerns, accepting with thanks the cup of coffee his wife placed before him. Taking the stopper from the whisky decanter, he dropped a dram into his cup and pushed the decanter across to Marcus.

Following suit, he offered it back to Arianna, but she declined with a smiling shake of her head, and it occurred to Marcus she hadn't had any wine with lunch either. Watching carefully, he saw the way her hand went unconsciously to her stomach, the look she exchanged with Luke, and the penny dropped with a resounding clang.

"Is there something you two aren't telling me?"

At their guilty faces, he raised an eyebrow, then looked pointedly at Arianna's stomach, enjoying the fluttery looks they traded, that silent communication network only husband and wife seem to be able to use.

"Well," Arianna began, with a coy smile. "We were going to wait to make the announcement until we got back off holiday, but as you've guessed it, yes, I'm ten weeks pregnant."

"Hey, that's amazing. Congratulations," beamed Marcus, genuinely thrilled at the news he was to be an uncle again. Lifting his cup, he toasted them in whisky enhanced coffee.

"To the pair of you, congratulations on your new arrival."

"I had to keep it a secret," Lucia was bouncing in her chair with excitement. "I'm going to have a little brother or sister."

Marcus glanced at Megan. Catching her at an unguarded moment, the naked hunger on her face took his breath away as she stared at Arianna longingly, Brewster cuddled fiercely to her cheek.

"When we get back from holiday I'm going to help with the nursery," declared Lucia. She stopped and looked at Megan. "Of course, you can help," she said and patted Megan on the arm. "It'll be fun, we can do it together."

Marcus exchanged shocked glances with the other adults.

"Lucia," Arianna said gently. "How did you know Megan wanted to help with the nursery?"

"I... I don't know." Lucia was uncomfortable with the way all three adults were looking at her.

"I thought she might like to, that's all. And she would, wouldn't you?"

She turned on Megan who visibly shrank in her chair. Seeing her discomfort, Marcus decided to change the subject and seized on the first thing that came into his mind.

"Went to see an interesting house last week. You two would have loved it. A classic, old, rambling Edwardian villa."

"Really?" Knowing of his search for a home for Megan, Arianna sat upright with interest. "What was it like?"

"Well, huge. I mean, *really* big, but it needs a lot of work doing to it. Oh, so much work. It'll cost a fortune to bring that place round."

"But would it be worth it?" Luke asked.

"Yeah," Marcus considered it. "I think so, I mean, the place is gorgeous, all original features, fireplaces, cornices, doors, the lot. Nothing has been touched and it has a good feel to it. Great kitchen extension at the back, but even that needs a bit of updating and the gardens wonderful. Totally overgrown of course, but they grow all their own fruit and veg. They have chickens, and bees, and an amazing treehouse."

"A treehouse?" Luke smiled, in fond memory.

"What were the people like?" asked Arianna.

"There's this crazy hippie woman, I mean, totally hippie, dreadlocks, nose piercing, tie-dyed clothes, bangles, and necklaces dripping from everywhere … you know the sort. But she was nice enough. Grace Lovejoy, that was her name."

"That's a great name," murmured Arianna.

"And she's got three kids. A pretty, teenage daughter called Zoey, and twin ten-year-old sons, Finley, and Connor." Marcus paused, chuckling in remembrance, then saw the look on Arianna's face.

Puzzled, he frowned at her. Following her sharp nod towards Megan, he looked to see Megan's face, alive with interest, turned towards him. Brewster dropped, forgotten, in her lap, her hands were clasped in anticipation as her whole body yearned in his direction.

~Chapter Eight~
"She just wants to meet them."

Confused, Marcus glanced wildly at Arianna. *Keep talking*, she mouthed.

"They sound very interesting. Tell us more about them," she said.

"Umm, they have an old dog called Badger, a husky. He was lying under a tree in the garden but was so fat and lazy he didn't even bark at me, so not much of a guard dog. And ... and ... they had chickens, big, fat, white fluffy hens that clucked like this."

Desperately, he did his best chicken impression, frantically flapping his arms, making Lucia shriek with delighted laughter.

Glancing at Megan he saw her face, animated for the first time since her parents' murder, her eyes shining with interest.

"And the boys were up the treehouse and they'd pulled the ladder up after them. Their mother ordered them to let it down, but they wouldn't. So, she told them to again, but do you know what that pair of naughty monkeys did?"

"What? What?" cried Lucia, clapping her hands. Peering at Megan, Marcus saw her sitting on the edge of her seat, and Brewster slip unnoticed to the floor.

"They threw a rotten tomato at me from the treehouse." Lucia screamed with laughter and Megan's eyes widened.

"They did what?" Luke stared. "Did it hit you?"

"Yep," grinned Marcus, wryly. "Got me right on the suit lapel."

"Oh no, not your suit," exclaimed Arianna. "Which one?"

"The Ralph Lauren."

"But that's your favourite, can it be cleaned?"

"Already has been." Marcus waved away her concern. "Besides, it doesn't matter, it's only a suit."

"Only a suit!"

Luke and Arianna exchanged stunned glances, smirks breaking out on their faces.

"Well," Luke continued, "I never thought I'd live to see the day when my brother, Marcus, uttered the words, 'it's only a suit'."

"So, are you going to make an offer for this house?" asked Arianna, once all the laughter had died down.

"No," Marcus replied. "It's too big and needs too much doing to it."

Silence fell over the table.

Megan reached down and retrieved Brewster, crawling back to the furthest reaches of her chair, the shutters descending once more over her eyes, and the spark of animation in her face being instantly extinguished as if someone had reached in and snuffed out her flame.

"Megan, honey," he looked down at her bowed head. "The house is too big and too old, and it needs so much work doing to it. It's not the home for us. I'll keep looking and we'll find it soon, I promise you we will."

She looked up at him, knocking him back with the pleading in her eyes.

"I think," Arianna began slowly. "Megan would like to help you look for your new home."

"Would you?" Marcus asked her. "Megan, do you want to look at the houses with me? Because if you want to, then that's fine. I'm sorry, I didn't think. I should have asked if you wanted to come along ..." he paused. Megan had gone again, back into herself.

"Megan, please ... tell me what you want, and I'll get it for you. Please, I'll do anything, just tell me what you want."

She looked at him. Stared right through him. Then carefully and precisely, she placed Brewster down safely in her lap, bent her arms at the elbow, and flapped them once, copying his earlier chicken imitation.

"You want to see the chickens?" he asked, his heart sinking.

A pause. She nodded. Once.

"But honey, if we go back to see the chickens it will give them hope that we want to buy the house, and that's not fair to them. They're a nice family, Megan, it wouldn't be fair..."

He stopped dead. On the word family, she leant forward and placed her hand on his cheek. He felt it cold against his skin.

To his dismay, a single tear slid down her small cheek as she simply looked at him, a world of wanting in her gaze.

Sending a 'help me' look in Arianna's direction, she merely shook her head, as lost as he was. Her hand clasped in Luke's, she seemed unable to help or advise, sadness at the situation etched into her features.

He glanced at Luke. His face sombre, Luke too shook his head, so no help coming from that direction either.

At last, he looked at Lucia. Meeting his gaze, she slid down from her chair and came to stand beside him, taking his hand in her small one.

"It's all right, Uncle Marcus, she understands you probably can't buy the house, but she still wants to see it. And the chickens, and Badger, and the treehouse, but most of all, she wants to see them."

"Them?" he queried in confusion,

"Them, the family, Grace and Zoey, and Finley, and Connor, she wants to see the Lovejoys, that's all. She just wants to meet them."

"Thank you so much for allowing us to come at such short notice." It was later that same evening. Leaving Luke's, Marcus had called the estate agent on a whim, catching them before they closed for the day.

He redirected the taxi when the estate agent called back moments later to confirm that yes, Ms Lovejoy was in, and yes, it was convenient for them to go for a second viewing.

After being dropped off in front of the house, Marcus was aware of Megan beside him, clutching Brewster.

Her eyes were wide, roaming over the front of the house, taking everything in, absorbing the bay windows, the impressive three-storey façade, the pattern of stone flowers set over the top windows, and the many chimneys jutting up to the sky.

"It's fine," replied Grace.

If she was shocked to see him again, she hid it well, her gaze instead travelling down to Megan.

"Well, hello," she said, her voice warm and welcoming. "What's your name?"

There was a beat, a pause, then Marcus said, "This is Megan. Megan, this is Ms Lovejoy."

"Oh, call me Grace," she laughingly insisted, stepping back to allow them entry.

The house seemed different this time, cosier, less grubby, friendlier. Stepping into its cool, shady interior Marcus felt the house put its arms around him, almost as if welcoming him back.

Stunned to feel Megan's small hand slip into his, he looked down at her and was delighted with the shy, warm smile she gave him. He tightened his grip and was rewarded when she squeezed his hand back.

"Where do you want to start?" Grace asked.

Marcus felt that subtle pressure on his palm again. "Well, this viewing is actually for Megan's sake, and I know she wants to see the garden."

"Cool," agreed Grace, and they followed her long-skirted, slim-hipped saunter down the hall.

Marcus caught the faint jingle of her ankle bells, and glancing down saw she was barefooted, her feet long and slender, her bony ankles caressed by her long skirts.

Entering the kitchen, three pairs of eyes looked up from the kitchen table where various bits of artwork and model aeroplane parts were scattered around.

Zoey smiled a welcome. The boys nervously grimaced, obviously still concerned about the possible state of his million-pound suit.

"Everyone, this is Megan. She's come to look at the garden."

"Hey, Megan," said Zoey. Pushing back her chair, she sauntered over, crouched to Megan's height, and tapped Brewster on the paw.

"He's awesome. What's his name?"

"This is Brewster," replied Marcus when Megan squirmed against his leg.

"Hey, cool name," declared Zoey casually. "He looks a lot like the little dog I have on my keychain..."

She stood up and reached for a backpack that was sprawled on the table, its contents spilling. Snapping a keychain off the strap she unthreaded a small, dog mascot from it.

"Here you go," she said, handing it to Megan.

Looking at it, Marcus saw the tiny dog did indeed look like a miniature version of Brewster.

Taking the toy, Megan peered at it, examining it from every angle, before bestowing a rare, shy smile on Zoey and holding it back up to her.

"Keep it," declared Zoey. "It can be Brewster's pal, kind of a Mini Brew."

She held out a hand to Megan.

"Would you like me to show you the garden?"

Megan hesitated, glancing up at Marcus as if asking for permission.

"If you'd like to go and look at the garden with Zoey, honey, that's fine," he said. Somehow, he trusted the tall girl with the old eyes and the calm aura.

Confidently, Megan let go of his hand and held it out to Zoey, who took it and beamed a warmly encouraging smile.

"Tell you what, it's the chickens' teatime. Would you like to feed them?"

Megan's eyes grew huge, and she nodded, following happily when Zoey led her to the door, shadowed by the twins. The adults watched them go, then Grace turned to Marcus with a knowing smile.

"Your daughter's a sweetie."

"She's not my daughter," Marcus replied. "She's my niece, although I have adopted her. She was my sister's daughter, but, oh," he sighed heavily, "it's a long story…"

Grace reached for a bottle on the counter and took a pair of glasses from a cupboard. Sitting at the table, she pushed out the chair opposite with her foot and poured wine from the bottle into both glasses.

Holding one out to him, she said,

"I've got time."

Marcus hesitated.

He didn't know this woman, but he had to talk to someone. His family were too close to the situation.

Oh, they listened, they cared, but somehow it felt wrong talking about his fears for Megan, admitting how angry he was at Monica, deep down inside, for getting herself killed and leaving him to deal with this.

Even though he knew how stupidly irrational and unfair it was, he still couldn't help but feel a tiny bit resentful at the unfairness of it all.

Sighing, he sat, took the wine she offered and gulped a mouthful.

He coughed.

Spluttered.

His spleen feeling like it was about to erupt through his windpipe, red-faced and wheezing, he finally managed to gasp, "What the hell …? What is that?!"

"Peapod and raisin," replied Grace calmly, seeming to find his discomfort amusing. "It's a bit of an acquired taste."

"I'll say," he drawled, eyeing the glass suspiciously, not sure about risking a second sip.

"Old Mr Branson two doors up makes it, and he trades with me for fresh fruit and veg."

"I see," replied Marcus, cautiously sniffing at the glass, the fumes alone smelling 100% proof.

"What did you ever do to him that he should hate you so?"

Grace chuckled and took a sip of her wine. Unfazed by its paint stripping tendencies, she leant back in her chair and fixed him with an enquiring gaze.

"So, Megan?"

"Megan," he agreed. "Where do I begin?"

"At the beginning?" she suggested.

So, he did.

~Chapter Nine~
"I've done crying over it."

When he stopped talking silence fell over the kitchen. Through the open door, twilight was seeping into the room, and Marcus could hear a bird singing outside.

There was movement as Badger waddled in, slumped his stout frame onto the rug, and promptly went to sleep. Marcus thought how peaceful it was here. How you would never imagine one of the largest, busiest cities in the world was a mere short taxi ride away.

Grace drew a deep, shuddering breath, and wiped a shaking hand over her eyes.

"That poor child," she murmured. "I can't imagine one of mine lying there, all night, after seeing ... What kind of a monster could do this?"

"At least he didn't kill Megan," he replied.

"No, I guess maybe some monsters have lines even they won't cross, but still, that poor child. No wonder she's not talking."

"So, I'm afraid we're here under false pretences. Although I love your house and think it could be amazing, it is simply too big for us. But, when I spoke about it, Megan got excited and interested, for the first time since ... and she wanted to meet you all. I don't know why, but something about you sparked her interest."

"Is it any wonder?" Grace asked, pouring them another glass. Marcus looked down in surprise.

Somehow, whilst telling his story, he had finished his wine. Maybe it *was* an acquired taste, he thought ruefully.

"That poor child lost everything in one night. Her parents, the life she knew, her home, her school, her friends, her country … everything. Perhaps hearing about a life completely different from the one she had, a cluttered, rambling old house compared to a sleek, modern New York apartment. A large, noisy, crazy family instead of being an only child. Perhaps the strangeness, the oddness of it all, made her stop thinking about it, if only for a while. Maybe it took her mind off it, and that's a good thing."

"Maybe," Marcus agreed, then looked at Grace, really looked at her. As dusk fell she lit the fat candle in the middle of the table, and in its forgiving glow, her eyes were soft and kind.

Unused to seeing a woman unmade up, he saw that what he considered plainness was a natural beauty, wholesome and real. The nose piercing twinkled in the candlelight but somehow, he didn't even mind that anymore.

"So, what's your story?" he began slowly, unable to believe he was having this discussion with a woman he didn't know. A woman so far off-type if he had seen her in the street, he would have dismissed her instantly as someone not worth knowing. Feeling small and shallow at such a reflection, he leant forward, sipping at his wine. Which was not bad once you got used to it.

"How did you end up here and now?"

"Here and now?" Grace mused. "Very poetic. I like it. Well, I was a bit of a wild child. My dad had left us, and mum struggled to cope with me. It was a mess, there was no money, so she turned to alcohol and drugs to get her through. Eventually, I was taken into care, which I hated." She paused, lost in memory.

"What happened then?" asked Marcus, fascinated by the peep into a life so different from his. A childhood of need and poverty compared to his pampered and privileged upbringing.

"What happened then?" Grace shrugged in resignation. "Zoey happened. I was stupid and naïve and fell in with the wrong crowd and went to the wrong kind of party. Before I knew it, my drink had been spiked, and oops, I was four months pregnant." She met his eyes and smiled sadly, waiting for his judgement.

It never came. Instead, Marcus topped up her wine, finishing the bottle. "That's tough," he murmured, shaking his head. "And the father?"

"Never came forward, and of course, I couldn't remember much about that night, so, well, that was that. Being young and stupid I didn't think I could be pregnant until I started to show, and one of the other girls noticed and reported it to the staff who had me tested. By then she was on her way, and it was too late to stop her."

"Did you consider adoption?"

"They all tried to persuade me it was for the best, but I couldn't. From the moment I felt her move inside me, I loved her. Giving her up was never an option. Maybe I wanted something all my own to love, to take care of. Someone to need me, rely on me," she smiled wistfully.

"I have never regretted keeping Zoey, not for one second. Never, not even when things were so tough, I was surviving on cornflakes. She is a child who was meant to be on this earth. I know, she's mine, so of course, I'm going to think she's special, but she is, she really is. There's something about her, she's just … Zoey…"

Marcus nodded, thinking about Zoey, her smile, her eyes, her instant connection with Megan, her kindness with her.

"And the boys?" he asked, a grin breaking out at the thought of them.

"Oh," Grace clapped a hand to her forehead. "Those two will be the death of me."

"Is their father still around?"

"No." The light went out of her face. Looking down at the table she picked at a rogue crumb. Rolling it absently between her fingers, she finally flicked it to the floor and looked back up at him, the sheen of tears evident in her eyes.

"Zoey and I were alone for three long years, then I met Daniel. Kind, amazing, crazy Daniel. I met him at a summer folk festival, he was one of the acts. We were sitting in the front row. Zoey was singing along and waving daisies at him. Afterwards, he came to find us, and that was that. It was love, instant and true. We were together until the day he left me, two years later."

"What happened?" Marcus asked into the silence, fascinated by this woman, by her story.

"He came into some money when his parents died, enough for a deposit on this place. It was the credit crunch, so property was cheap. We fell in love with it, planned to do it up and maybe open a bed and breakfast for people who wanted to stay somewhere more homelike, more natural. We did the kitchen extension, and then I found out I was pregnant. Daniel was over the moon, asked me to marry him immediately. Of course, I agreed, I'd never been so happy."

Grace paused, took a deep breath and an even deeper gulp of her wine.

"On the day of the wedding, he popped out in the van to get my bouquet. I wasn't going to have one, the expense you know, but secretly he'd arranged one, so he slipped out whilst I was getting ready. He didn't say where he was going, so I never knew until later, where he'd gone and why. I only knew he was gone. We were supposed to be getting married and he was gone."

Grace shrugged, and a world of suffering was conveyed in that one, simple gesture.

"I sat there waiting for him to come back. I was still waiting in my wedding dress when the police knocked on the door."

Marcus felt his heart clench, moved beyond belief at the sadness of her life, made even more shocking by the simple, stark way she told it.

"How did…?" He was unsure how to continue.

"He die?" Grace glanced at him, and her mouth quirked. "One of those stupid, random acts that make you seriously wonder if the universe has any plan or reason at all. A taxi driver was late picking up a fare. He ran a red light and went straight into him. Daniel's neck was broken in the impact. He died instantly."

"I'm so sorry," said Marcus, feeling the inadequacy of his words, but unsure what else to say or do.

"It's all right," Grace reached over and touched his hand. "Honestly, it's all right. It was a long time ago, and I've done crying over it. It sometimes gets to me though. The sheer waste of his life. I mean, was that it? All his life, all he had done, all he was, just for it to end like that. It seems such a waste."

"Yes," Marcus agreed, thinking of Monica, of Walter. "It does."

"Anyway," Grace pulled her hand away leaving him bereft. "We've been getting by on the rest of Daniel's inheritance, the little I manage to earn from various jobs, and benefits ever since then. But the savings are all gone, swallowed up by the house, so now it must be sold."

"I'm sorry," Marcus murmured again, gripped by an irresistible urge to offer to buy the house, give her money, anything to make her life a little easier and put the sparkle back into her eyes.

Grace shrugged expressively, stretched back in her chair, and looked around the darkening kitchen as if startled by the passage of time.

"Goodness," she exclaimed. "What time is it? We've been talking so long I completely lost track of time. Those kids will be wanting their supper."

"Yes," agreed Marcus. "I need to get Megan home for hers."

"Kids," said Grace. "They're awfully quiet. I don't hear anything. Can you hear anything?"

"No, should we be worried?"

"If Zoey wasn't with them, then yes, I'd be worried, but as she is, no. She's a natural with children. That's what she wants to do when she's older, work with special needs children. I think she'll be good at it."

"Yes," Marcus agreed again, remembering Zoey's patience and gentleness with Megan. "I think she will be too."

Following Grace out into the magical twilight evening, Marcus noticed little solar lights flicking on all over the garden. He thought again what a special place it was, how sheltered and protected it felt. As if the worries and cares of the outside world could never breach its wooden perimeters.

Approaching the treehouse, Marcus saw lights glowing through its window, heard a contented clucking from the chicken coop as he passed. He imagined all those happy, over-fed hens curled up asleep, or however, it was chickens slept.

"Zoey?" Grace stood at the bottom of the ladder and called softly up into the branches. "It's time for Megan to go home now."

Amidst a chorus of boyish "Aw noes," which floated down on the evening air, Zoey's head appeared in the window.

"Now? We haven't finished the story yet."

"Well, she must go home for her supper, and it's quite a taxi ride home for them. The poor little mite will be starving if they stay much longer."

There was silence for a while as if Zoey were contemplating the problem.

"Can't they stay for supper?" came the logical response. Grace looked at Marcus. In the dusky half-light, he saw her rueful grin.

"It's probably a great deal humbler than you're used to, no champagne and caviar I'm afraid, but it's homegrown, home-cooked and there's plenty of it so you're more than welcome to stay."

"Oh no, I mean, we couldn't possibly put you out," Marcus politely insisted, surprised by how much he wanted to stay.

"Look," she again took his hand in hers. He felt her closeness, could smell her earthy, womanly scent, see her eyes glinting in the dim light. "Why don't we drop the whole pretence that you're going to buy my house. You know you're not going to. I know, you're not going to. You know, I know, you're not going to. Good. Now that's out of the way that leaves us, two single parents, facing an evening alone with our kids."

She softly laughed in the balmy stillness of the perfect evening. "That's daft. We have plenty of food. I can even rustle up another bottle of wine. Why not share the evening, let the kids stay together? It'll be good for my brood, and I think it will be good for Megan. So, what do you say?"

Marcus hesitated, and Grace shook his arm. "Don't be so stubborn," she insisted. "I know you want to stay, that it's only politeness and worry about eating into our resources that's making you hesitate, but I promise you, we're not quite in the workhouse yet, and it is only supper."

"Okay." Marcus thought about the empty apartment that awaited them, the struggle of cooking supper for them both and sitting there in silence, watching Megan push hers around a plate. With no Delphine to even share the burden of quietness, it was not an evening he was particularly looking forward to.

"Thank you," he said.

"Great. Kids!" Grace called up into the tree. "Come down and wash for supper, then you can all help get it ready, Megan's staying."

Amid a chorus of whoops and cheers from above, she grinned at him again. "Look, if it makes you feel any better, we can say next time supper is on you. Deal?" She held out her hand and he took it, feeling the smallness of her bones, the rough texture of workworn palms.

"Deal," he agreed, and warmth spread throughout his body at her touch.

~Chapter Ten~
"Mommy, please wake up, please."

A week later, Marcus was blessing the strange set of circumstances that had brought the Lovejoys into their lives. That first evening – that amazing, relaxing supper eaten mostly by candlelight, with the soft music of some local indie band seeping from an ancient stereo system – was one he would never forget.

The food had been simple but wholesome. Homemade bread with boiled eggs collected fresh from the chickens that day, jacket potatoes cooked in foil with butter and salt, their skins crisp and utterly delicious.

Goat's cheese bartered for with a fellow allotment keeper, tangy and sharp, to be melted into the potatoes, spread on bread, or crumbled with fingers directly into open mouths.

Fresh salad and tomatoes bursting with flavour, a round of laughter being evoked when Marcus threatened to throw them at the boys.

Bowls of preserved raspberries, strawberries, and redcurrants, great clots of cream to be dolloped onto each bowlful. And wine, blackberry this time, its alcohol edged sweetness making his taste buds tingle.

Relaxing for the first time in forever, Marcus watched Megan. She didn't speak, that would be too much to hope for, but she smiled, watching the Lovejoys as they interacted as a family, the boys mildly bickering until Grace silenced them with a look.

She almost laughed at the silly jokes and banter that flew across the table, her eyes shining and her whole face lighting up.

Pleased to see her happy and engaged, his eyes would meet Grace's in silent communion, the shared pleasure passing between them.

Going home that evening and having to leave the magical, inclusive glow of the candle warm kitchen had been quite a wrench.

The Lovejoys lined up on the doorstep to see them off, Megan waving until the taxi turned the corner and they could be seen no more.

Upon reaching his apartment and switching on the lights, Marcus winced away from its brightness. Looking at the stark, contemporary blandness of everything, he understood what Delphine had meant about it not being a home.

Now it was the following week, and he and Megan were on their way to supper at the Lovejoys again. The food, this time, was provided by them.

They wandered Harrods food hall, Marcus allowing Megan to pick what she thought they might enjoy, his brows lifting at the eclectic collection of tasty food she chose, wondering what the others would make of it.

Driving this time because Marcus had an early morning conference call the next day, they edged their way through Saturday afternoon traffic.

Looking in the rear-view mirror he saw Megan, safely strapped in her car seat, watching with interest all the different cultures that passed outside the car windows.

He glanced up at the sky. The weather had been strange all week, unpredictable and changeable. Veering wildly from bright sunshine one moment to torrential downpours the next, and the black-edged clouds looming above made him suspect they were in for another soaking.

The radio beeped the hour and he realised they were early. He hoped that would be okay, then had to switch his wipers on as the heavens opened and rain lashed at the windscreen.

"Goodness! Look at this, Megan," he remarked, glancing at her again in the mirror as she pressed Brewster's front paw to the window.

"It's really coming down hard, isn't it?"

She met his gaze in the mirror, her lips parted slightly, and she bobbed her head. Not much, but it was communication, an acknowledgement of his words.

Grinning to himself, Marcus changed gear, indicated, and turned onto the high street of the area where the Lovejoys lived.

"Nearly there," he commented, then jumped as Megan began tapping frantically on her window. He glanced over his shoulder at her in concern.

"What's up, Megan?" he asked and followed her pointed finger, seeing them as well. Grace and Zoey, both soaked to the skin, laughing at the rain, and clutching each other as they ran, bags in hand.

Scanning traffic, indicating his intention to pull over, Marcus pressed the button to wind down the passenger's side window. Leaning over, he called.

"Need a lift?"

Looking around, Grace saw him, her face breaking into a smile of welcome relief.

"Thank you," she gasped, as she and Zoey scrambled into the car. "It just suddenly came down! What a summer it's been, so changeable."

Marcus smiled, concentrating on pulling back out into traffic. In the mirror he saw Zoey do up her seat belt, exchanging fist bumps with Megan as she taught her last time. Zoey laughed, patted Brewster on the head, and touched Mini Brew safely chained to Brewster's collar.

Grace was wiping at her damp arms and face, her skimpy vest top almost transparent from the rain, her long skirt clinging moistly to her legs. Aware of her slender body, so close he could have reached over and touched it, Marcus frowned. Where the hell had that come from?

Grace was so not his type, the whole hippie, earth mother look having never done anything for him. No, he appreciated Grace as a woman and a friend. A kind, generous, big-hearted woman who was helping his child come back from a very dark place.

Slowing down at traffic lights, Marcus jumped back into the moment as two young men pounced at the car, squirting cleaning fluid over the windows, and scraping at non-existent dirt.

Annoyed, he tried to wave them away, but one leapt to the back, spraying Megan's window, and grinning maniacally through the glass at her.

Megan screamed.

Not a shocked, little girl scream, but a spine-chilling, bowel-loosening, horror movie scream.

Startled, Marcus and Grace twisted in their seats, and Zoey shrank, wide-eyed, from the demented, tormented child who thrashed and twisted in her car seat.

Straining frantically against the restraints, her eyes rolled, white and terrified, as her hands ripped at her hair.

"No," she howled, in a low gruff voice. "No ... no ... no .... don't talk, don't talk, don't talk .... don't tell, don't tell. Don't tell anyone, little girl, don't tell ... don't tell..."

"Megan!" cried Marcus. "What is it?"

Zoey had recovered her senses enough to slide back across the seat. Struggling with the car seat straps she managed to snap them open, pulling Megan into her lap, fighting to contain the thrashing arms, the flailing legs.

"Just drive!" she ordered, receiving a slap from the feral, fighting frenzy she was struggling to hold. "DRIVE!" she yelled when he hesitated.

Fumbling in his trouser pocket, Marcus found a tenner, opened the window a crack and threw it at the shocked man outside. Gunning the engine as the lights changed, they shot forward into traffic.

"Don't tell!" Megan screamed, her body arching in Zoey's grasp. "I'll kill you if you tell. Mustn't tell, must never, ever, tell! Do you want to end up like your mommy and daddy?"

Marcus and Grace exchanged horrified glances. Behind them, Zoey was shushing and soothing, her eyes huge and meeting theirs in the dawning realisation that Megan was re-living the carjacking, was experiencing again the murder of her parents.

"Mommy!" howled Megan. "Daddy! No, no, no, please ... no, please no, don't..."

Her voice dropped to a whisper, as she twisted in Zoey's arms and stared at nothing. Her eyes were huge. Her pupils fathomless, black pits.

"Mommy, Mommy, please wake up, please, Daddy, please …"

Marcus's skin crawled in horror.

"Marcus…" whispered Grace, clutching at his arm. He nodded, his brain racing with the importance of what they were hearing.

Megan's body bucked in Zoey's grasp. Panting, she grabbed Zoey's arms, her voice again taking on a gruff, low tone almost as if, Marcus realised, she was repeating the attacker's words exactly as they had sounded to her seven-year-old ears.

"Don't talk … don't talk to anyone … don't talk at all … if you do, if you tell, if you talk, I'll find you, I can always find you … and I'll kill you, you hear that little girl if you talk, I'll kill you."

Megan's body bucked in Zoey's arms.

"MOMMY!" she screamed again, then collapsed, her eyes wide and blank, great, gasping heaving breaths filling the car as she struggled for air.

In the sudden, stunned silence, Zoey held her, smoothing her hair, cuddling her trembling body.

"It's okay," she promised. "It's all going to be okay. You're safe now; nothing can hurt you. You're safe, I promise you. No one will ever hurt you again."

"Let's get her home," Grace softly ordered. "We'll deal with it there."

Marcus nodded, thinking how strange it was that when she said home, he automatically thought of hers, not his.

~Chapter Eleven~
"She has to talk now, doesn't she?"

Reaching the Lovejoys house, Marcus carried a limp and pliant Megan indoors, the boys rushing to meet them, their curious exclamations and questions hastily hushed by Grace. Promising to tell them everything later, they were sent to retrieve the supper from the car. Eyes greedy at the thought of food, they hurried to comply, and Marcus sat on the old sofa in the corner of the kitchen cuddling Megan's damp body to his chest.

Zoey sat beside him, her calm and steady hands stroking Megan's hair, soothing, and relaxing her, until Megan's eyelids drooped, and she drifted into an exhausted sleep, wrung out by the shocking events. Gently, Marcus eased her down onto the sofa, and Zoey covered her with a blanket.

Softly, they retreated to the furthest reaches of the kitchen, conferring in urgent whispers.

"It was that man," said Zoey. "The man who tried to clean her window. She took one look at him and that seemed to trigger her memories of what happened to her parents."

Marcus glanced at Grace.

"Zoey knows?"

"Just Zoey," Grace reassured. "I knew she'd understand, but I didn't tell the boys."

"Didn't tell us what?" a pair of strident voices demanded. Hastily, Grace shushed them again, her and Zoey taking the bags of food from them.

"Megan's been through a bad time," their mum explained. "She saw her parents killed in front of her, their car was stolen, and for some reason, no one knows why the carjackers shot them in front of Megan. That's why she doesn't talk right now."

The boys exchanged looks; their boisterous natures subdued.

"We'll help protect her," they promised Marcus, standing taller with the importance of their self-imposed mission. "If the bad guys come after Megan, we'll protect her."

"Be quiet, silly boys," hissed Zoey. "She was startled by car cleaners on the high street, that's all. It made her remember, made her start talking again. Her parents were killed over in America; no one's going to come after Megan here.

"They might," pouted Finley, or it could have been Connor. His twin nodded earnestly.

"Finn's right, they might come after her, especially now she's talking again and can identify them."

"Thank you, boys," said Marcus, solemnly. "It's good to know I can depend on you to protect Megan should I ever not be around."

The boys straightened even further.

"I wonder," began Grace. "Do you think it was only the noise and fuss of the car cleaners that startled her? Or was there something about them? The one who tried to clean her window, I didn't see him. What did he look like, Zoey?"

Zoey considered.

"Well, he was young, dark. He looked Spanish, Portuguese, something like that. He had one of those silly boy band beards, you know," her hands gestured to her chin, "that little tuft they have in the middle. And he was wearing a dark beanie pulled down almost to his eyes."

"Maybe one of the carjackers looked like that," suggested Grace, and looked at Marcus. "This could be important. I think you should let the police in charge of the case know."

"Yes," he agreed, sighing as a wave of exhaustion drenched him. "But tomorrow, not tonight. Tonight, I think we should enjoy our supper. I don't know about you, but I'm starving, and I could really, *really* do with a drink."

He pulled out his phone and began texting.

Grace frowned. "Thought you were driving?"

"I was. Is it okay if we leave the car here, get a taxi home and collect it tomorrow?"

"Of course, but what about that conference call thingy you said you had?"

Pressing send, Marcus grinned at her. "I've asked my PA to rearrange it for another time."

"On a Saturday? You bothered the poor woman on a Saturday?"

"Sally's not a woman, she's Sally. Besides, I pay her an awful lot of money to let me bother her on a Saturday if I need to. Right," he pulled a bottle of wine out. "Corkscrew?"

When it became clear Megan wasn't going to wake up anytime soon, they ate. Leaving ample for her to have should she be hungry when she awoke, they rummaged through the Harrods bags, the boys' eyes widening at the myriad of exotic and expensive foods Grace pulled out and arranged on the table.

Talking quietly amongst themselves, Marcus poured Grace a glass of wine and watched her take a small sip, her eyes showing her appreciation.

"Oh, my goodness," she murmured. "No wonder you choked on my homemade stuff. This is amazing."

"It was fine," he said. "Once I got used to it."

Grace laughed and poured a small glass for Zoey, who took a sip, nodding her approval.

After supper, Marcus helped Grace to clear away, the boys having mysteriously vanished at this point.

Zoey wandered over to the sofa. Curling up on the other end, she lay her head on its arm and simply watched Megan sleep.

"Megan sleeps more than Badger," one of the twins had commented over dinner.

"Don't be stupid," his brother had retorted. "Nothing sleeps more than Badger."

Looking at the fat creature asleep on the hearthrug, Marcus had been inclined to agree.

"Do you think she'll start talking now?" Grace asked quietly, eyes warm and concerned in the candlelight. Her face was resting on one hand as she leant on the table and her auburn dreadlocks over one shoulder, she looked the same age as Zoey. Her cheeks were flushed from the wine – they were onto the second bottle by now – and Marcus wondered how he could have ever considered her plain.

"I don't know," he sighed. "I hope so, but I'm afraid if I tell the police this then they'll want to interview her, will want her to see a police artist.

I'm scared of what that will do to her. She's so fragile, so damaged, I don't want her upset."

"I know," Grace agreed quietly, as she considered the matter. "But that man killed her parents. He should be brought to justice for that; you can't let him get away with it. Maybe he'll kill again, take some other innocent life. Think about how you'd feel. Think of how Megan will feel when she's old enough to understand. Hard as it is, Marcus, I don't think you have a choice in this."

"I know," he agreed, rubbing at tired eyes. "I know." He glanced at Megan, still asleep on the sofa, her small body exhausted by her earlier outburst. "I guess I should call a taxi. Try and get her home."

"No," said Zoey. "She's staying here tonight. She can sleep in my bed. It's a double, so it's big enough."

Marcus looked at Grace, who shrugged.

"Fine by me," she murmured. "You can stay too if you like. There's plenty of room. I can easily make you up a bed...."

It was late, gone midnight. The boys had been packed off to bed hours before, appeased by the promise that Megan would be there for breakfast. Zoey and Megan too had gone to bed.

Zoey led the way to her room, and Marcus carried Megan's soft, light body up the stairs into a large, artistically decorated room, gently placing her on the wrought iron bed.

"It's okay," Zoey assured him. "I have a t-shirt she can sleep in. I'll take care of her. Don't worry."

"Thanks, Zoey," he murmured. "For everything, thank you."

She looked at him in the dim glow of the bedside lamp, looking so much like her mother he had a glimpse of what Grace had been like at her age. Her smile was gentle as she stroked Megan's hair.

"It's all right. She needs a bit of help, that's all. It's a lot for a little girl to have gone through. I think whoever killed her parents threatened her, told her if she ever talked about it, ever told anyone what he looked like, then he'd find her and kill her too."

She sat on the edge of the bed and looked at him, her eyes full of knowledge beyond her years.

"It was all too much for her to handle, too much for her poor little mind to process, so it was easier for her not to talk at all."

Marcus was astounded at her wisdom, her grasp of the situation. "Yes," he nodded slowly. "I think you're right. I think that's what happened."

"But she has to talk now, doesn't she?"

"Yes," he agreed. "She has to now…"

Downstairs with Grace again he felt himself unwinding in her undemanding, soothing presence. They drank wine, talked some more, but mostly were silent and still, the barely audible music she put on washing over him like sensory anaesthesia.

He looked around the dimly lit kitchen, no longer noticing the mess or clutter, instead seeing only a home, a well-loved and much lived-in home.

He realised how much he wanted this now.

How much he had been missing out on all these years. How much he needed a home, not only for Megan but for him too.

"Thank you," he said, twirling his now empty glass by its stem.

"What for?" she asked, slightly startled.

"For everything, for last week, for tonight, for letting us stay, for letting us be a part, if only for a little while, of your amazing family. Thank you for your help and advice with Megan. Thank you for your fantastic kids, for Zoey. Thank you ... for being you."

She smiled, slow and steady. It warmed him right through, like the finest whisky, and he felt himself smiling back.

Reaching out, he put his hand over hers, feeling a spark of static as their skin brushed, heard her gasp of indrawn breath.

She stared at their joined hands.

For a pulse, a beat of his heart, she let her hand lie under his, then slowly, carefully, she withdrew it.

"You're welcome," she said, her smile now bright and forced. She stifled a yawn.

"Oh, it's so late," she added. "I think, maybe, we should go to bed."

His heart stopped. Did she mean...?

"I'll get some fresh sheets from the airing cupboard," she continued, and his body stood down again, his brain surprised at how disappointed he was.

How much had he been wondering what it would be like to lie next to her in her large bed upstairs? To hear the chime of the small chain of bells draped around the bedstead as he took her in his arms, kissed her lips, ran his hands over her body.

Stop it, he told himself. This woman is too nice to play fast and loose with.

She is your friend.

She is a good person.

Not the sort to use in a one-night stand, and then discard the next day.

After all, it's not as if you're interested in her, is it...

Is it?

~Chapter Twelve~
"Poor little mite,"

The sobbing scream erupted into the night. Almost expecting it after the traumas of the day, Marcus rolled over in the bed and hit the floor running. Snatching up his trousers from the floor, he thrust one leg in, then the other, reaching the door as he did up his fly, fumbling with the door handle.

Wrenching the door open, he headed for Zoey's room as the next scream cut into the echo of the first. Skidding around the corner he collided with Grace, stumbling sleepy-eyed and zombie-like from her room.

She grunted as he cannoned into her. Clutching at him to steady herself, he felt her warm hands on his arms as her body, clad only in a crop top and sleep shorts, bounced off his bare chest.

"Wah?" she gasped in shock. "What's happening?"

"Megan."

Strangely reluctant to let go, Marcus steadied her, a part of his brain noticing the well-toned muscular legs, the glimpse of the flat, bare stomach under the hem of the crop top.

Drawing herself away, Grace reached behind her door and pulled down a robe. Shoving her arms in, she pushed past him to Zoey's door from behind which great, gasping cries could be heard, and the soothing rumble of Zoey's voice.

Tapping gently, Grace waited until they heard a low invitation to enter, then eased the door open and peered around the corner.

"Everything okay, love?"

"Yes," Zoey's calm voice reassured. Craning to see over Grace's shoulder, Marcus caught a glimpse of a tangle of Megan curled up in Zoey's arms, sucking Brewster's paw, being rocked, and shushed. "Just a bad dream, but she's okay now. Me and Brewster, we've got this covered. Go back to bed."

"Okay love, is there anything you need?"

"No, we're fine, thanks, Mum. Night."

"All right, night love, see you both in the morning." Easing the door shut, Grace turned and looked at him. In the dim light, he could see the concern in her eyes, the soft worry on her face. "Poor little mite," she murmured.

"I am so sorry," he began, but she shook her head, and when he opened his mouth to speak again, put her finger to his lips.

"The boys," she murmured and moved silently to another door. Easing it open a crack, she peered around into the dimly lit room, then quietly backed out, softly closing the door.

"Both still sound asleep," she whispered and smiled at him. "Those two would sleep through an atom bomb hitting the house."

Marcus smiled back and the moment stretched as he became intensely aware of them standing there, in the middle of the night, half-dressed, simply looking at each other.

"I don't know about you," said Grace, slowly, "but I could do with a hot chocolate. After being woken up like that, it's going to be ages before I can get back to sleep. Would you like one?"

"Hot chocolate?" Marcus tried to remember the last time he had had a hot chocolate, probably not since being a child himself.

"Umm, yes, great, thank you."

Following her downstairs, he marvelled how her dreadlocks looked the same as they did during the day and appreciated the practicality of them.

He thought about Sullivan, one of Luke's operatives, who also had an impressive headful of dreadlocks. Marcus realised he had always made assumptions about those who sported them. Assumptions he now saw were wrong and unfair.

Going into the dark kitchen, Grace flicked on an old, battered Tiffany lamp that stood on the work surface near the Aga stove, and lit the large candle that was always a permanent fixture in the centre of the table. On the rug in front of the Aga where he was lying for warmth, Badger lifted his head in mute enquiry.

"It's all right, boy," Grace murmured, fondling his soft ears. Mumbling in response, Badger lay back down his weary head and closed his eyes.

Getting milk from the fridge, Grace measured out two mugs full into a saucepan and set it to boil. Taking a bar of dark chocolate from the cupboard, she broke off several squares and shared them equally between the mugs.

Intrigued, Marcus leant on the worktop, watching her. She glanced at him, smiled, then turned her attention back to the milk.

"Does she often get these nightmares?"

"Sometimes, although in the beginning, they were much worse. She would have several in one night. She's been so much better lately, I never thought… although I suppose I should have done, considering what happened today."

"Yes, it's no wonder she had a nightmare, poor little mite, re-living it all over again."

"Do you think Zoey's okay?"

"She'll be fine, there's no one better to cope with this. I told you, this is what Zoey wants to do. She's a natural at helping people, making them feel better."

"She must get it from her mother," he said, unthinkingly, then swallowed as Grace turned startled eyes up to him.

"I mean, you're so kind. You always seem to want to help people. Look at how amazing you've been to me and Megan."

"I've done nothing…"

"Yes, you have, you've brought that child out of her shell. I was beginning to despair of ever reaching her, but being here with you, and the kids, and the garden and the treehouse, and the chickens and, oh, everything, I've seen her change, get better, begin to come back to us, and … and… I wanted to say, thank you."

She looked at him, her eyes soft and dark in the dim light. Faltering into silence, Marcus shut up, unable to think of anything else to say, anything else to do. He merely stood there, staring back at her.

Wanting so much. Unsure of what it was he wanted. The woman? Or the moment? And afraid, so afraid of rejection, of getting it wrong.

The moment stretched into infinity. Aware of the rapid rise and fall of her chest beneath the flimsy dressing gown, Marcus couldn't help it, couldn't stop himself.

Trembling, he reached out a hand and gently touched her cheek, stroking it downwards, cupped her throat, then her shoulder.

Still, she said nothing, did nothing, to encourage him. Said nothing, did nothing, to stop him.

Gathering up all his courage he moved closer, bent forward until his forehead rested against hers. Sighing, he closed his eyes. Feeling her breath soft and sweet on his lips, he edged forward blindly until they touched.

Mouth to mouth. Then gently, oh so gently, and slowly, he kissed her.

Never had a kiss mattered so much. Never had so much been sought for, so much been asked for, so much been begged for.

Her arms crept around his waist, pulling him closer until he felt the whole, slim length of her body pressing against his, straining to get closer.

Groaning, he deepened the kiss, his hands moving down her back to hold her tightly.

It was so right, so very, very...

What was that smell?!

Burning, acrid...

They jumped apart as boiling milk spilt over the top of the pan and scorched on the hob, filling the air with the stench of burning milk.

Muttering an exclamation, Grace snatched the pan off the ring and thrust it into the sink. Grabbing a damp cloth, she wiped at the top of the Aga. Her cheeks flushed rosy-red as she avoided looking at him, her back expressing her mortification at what they had … what she'd…

"I'm sorry," she said, her voice low and steady. "I think hot chocolate is off the menu tonight. Perhaps it's best if we just go back to bed."

Nodding, Marcus stepped away to give her more room. Relieved it hadn't gone any further. For heaven's sake, after all, what the hell had he been playing at? Yet, at the same time, disappointed.

"No problem," he muttered to her stiff back after what seemed a lifetime of awkward silence. "I'll see you in the morning, night."

"Night," she mumbled in reply, her back still stubbornly turned against him, as she busied herself cleaning up the mess. He hovered uncertainly for a second longer, then took himself dejectedly off to bed.

~Chapter Thirteen~
"I want them to catch him,"

Next morning, Marcus woke abruptly. After getting back into bed he had tossed and turned for a few minutes, analysing over and again that impossible, logic-defying kiss.

He had then been surprised to slip into a deep sleep, to now awaken refreshed and alert, feeling like he had had the best night's sleep ever.

Must be something in the air, he thought, or maybe it was all that wine.

Taking the towel Grace had thoughtfully hung on the back of the bedroom door, he padded into the large bathroom.

Fiddling around with the ancient shower controls, he managed to coax a jet of water out of it and clambered in.

Five minutes later he staggered out, awakened fully and rather brutally by the shower's tendency to rudely blast him with freezing water.

Pulling his clothes back on from the previous night, he wondered what time it was and if anyone else was up yet.

Back in his room, he strapped on his watch, noting it was only just gone seven.

Creeping downstairs, he was drawn by the enticing aroma of coffee coming from the kitchen. Eagerly following his nose, he found a coffee pot wrapped snugly in an old tartan cover with a note propped against it, bearing the words, 'please help self'.

Obeying instructions, he found a large, pleasingly chunky coffee cup in one of the cupboards and inhaling the fumes wandered out the already open kitchen door.

Drawn by the sound of voices, he found all the Lovejoys and Megan busy in the vegetable plot. Pausing to sip his coffee, he watched as they all toiled away.

Grace was turning up tall, green plants, deploying an ancient fork with dexterity.

To his fascination, each forkful revealed potatoes, dozens on each plant, which she pulled up, shook the dirt off and dumped into a bucket beside her.

Zoey was crouched at the other end neatly pulling carrots from the dark earth, shaking, and dropping each orange spear into a basket.

Even the boys were busy picking runner beans. One either side of Megan, they were showing her which ones were the right size to pick, encouraging her as her small hands eagerly grasped and pulled.

Glancing up, Grace saw him and paused to rest on her fork. Pushing her dreadlocks back with a grubby hand, she left a streak of dirt on her cheek.

"Well, hello sleepyhead," she exclaimed.

Her gaze met his, steady and innocent, and Marcus realised, both with a sinking heart and a surge of relief, exactly how she wished to play it.

Kiss? What kiss?

Nothing happened.

We're fine, we're friends, that's all, just friends.

He gave an almost imperceptible nod and saw the relief that flooded her features, her smile now genuinely warm and welcoming.

The others looked up, and Marcus was cheered by the big beaming smile Megan gave him.

"Good morning," he replied. "What are you picking, Megan?" he asked, crossing over and peering into her nearly full basket.

"Beans," she said, and his heart stopped.

"Really? What type of beans are they?" he asked casually, not showing any reaction to the fact she'd spoken.

Megan paused and considered, her head on one side.

"Running beans," she declared and dropped another fat one into the basket.

"What can I do to help?" he asked, and Grace looked around, frowning.

"We've almost done, but I tell you what, maybe you and Megan could see if the chickens have left us any nice eggs for breakfast today."

Marcus held out a hand to his niece.

"How about it, Megan? Want to help me look for eggs?"

"Yes," she said and took his hand.

Unlatching the coop, they let themselves in, carefully refastening the door behind them. Aware he was trampling on chicken poop in his £400 shoes, Marcus found he didn't care.

As excited as a boy, he and Megan carefully searched the pen and coop, the chickens fussing around them.

Scooping out a pot of their feed, Megan tossed it to them, laughing as they scuttled over one another to get to it.

"Funny," she said, and Marcus smiled at her.

"Yes, they are funny," he agreed.

Emerging triumphantly from the coop, they proudly displayed the basketful of eggs they had collected to the others.

"Wow," exclaimed Grace. "Omelettes for breakfast for everyone then."

Marcus retrieved his empty cup from where he'd left it.

"Great coffee," he said. "Thank you."

"No, thank you," Grace laughed. "It was in the bag of food you brought yesterday."

He looked around admiringly, at the bulging baskets, boxes, and sacks of produce they had harvested from their small plot.

"This is all very impressive," he said. "What will you do with it all?"

"Some is for barter," said Grace, dumping the last of the potatoes in the bucket.

"I trade fresh fruit and veg for goat's cheese and butter, wine, bacon, and sausages with the neighbours and the local butcher."

Grace looked about at the garden, at her family busy harvesting the fruits of her labour.

"The rest we will store for winter. Some will be frozen and some, like the potatoes, will be stored in the shed."

Marcus nodded, reflecting how he had never thought before about where his food came from. It was all either delivered, or he wandered the food hall at Harrods.

He never stopped to think that it had to be grown, tended, and harvested. He looked at

Grace again, his admiration for her thriftiness increasing.

"You said you had an allotment. Is that ready for harvesting as well?"

"Almost," Grace confirmed. "I planted a week later there to give me some breathing space, but everything's ready, so in the next few days it'll be all hands to the decks to get the harvest in." She wiped her hands down her camo cargo pants.

"Right," she declared. "Breakfast." And there was a cheer of agreement from the others.

The next day Marcus phoned the police in New York and spoke to the inspector in charge of the case. He told him Megan was speaking again, of the incident in the car, and what she had said.

The man listened and agreed it was likely the car cleaner had reminded Megan of the carjacker.

He would fly over with a police artist he usually worked with, who would try to get an accurate drawing based on Megan's description.

Don't worry, the inspector reassured, he's a professional used to dealing with children and unreliable witnesses. If anyone could get an accurate description out of Megan, it would be him.

He had a few things to clear up, then they would come over, probably mid-week, but certainly by the weekend.

Marcus hung up, then thought about the weekend they had shared with the Lovejoys, and the light in Megan's face as she interacted with them, seeming a part of their family.

He thought about exposing her to the police again, dredging up the past for her, imagining the light being extinguished in her eyes.

He hated himself for what he was going to put her through, but ultimately knew Grace was right, he had no choice.

Sally buzzed into his thoughts.

"I have your mother on line one, Marcus."

Sighing, he reached for the phone.

"Hi, Mum."

"Marcus, darling. How is Megan? Is there any change?"

"Actually, Mum, there is."

Swiftly, he told her of the events of the weekend, of the fact Megan was talking again, albeit not proper sentences, merely words, but at least she was speaking and communicating with him.

Delphine had returned late Sunday, concerned at what had occurred but delighted when Megan had shyly said hello to her.

Hugging the little girl to her, she looked at Marcus over Megan's shoulder, relief and apprehension mingled in her gaze.

"Oh my," his mother exclaimed. "Do you think Megan will be able to give an accurate description of this man?"

"Maybe. Perhaps," Marcus said and listened to his mother take a deep, shuddering breath at the other end of the line.

"Mum?"

There was silence, then Marcus heard her crying again.

"Oh, Marcus," she sobbed. "I want them to catch him, catch whoever shot my baby girl. I want to see him punished for what he did. He killed my Monica over a car, he deserves to suffer for that. I could kill him myself for it."

She paused, took a deep, gulping breath and it struck Marcus that how he felt about Megan was how his mother had felt about Monica.

That no matter how grown-up, anal, and controlling Monica had become, to their mother, at least, she would always be her little girl.

"Would you like to come for a visit, Mum?" he asked, surprising himself.

There was a stunned silence.

"Really? You're inviting me to visit?"

"Yes."

Marcus felt mean for not having asked before. After all, Megan was her granddaughter, her only grandchild.

"Why don't you come over this weekend? I know Megan would love to see you, and she'll be a little down. Delphine leaves for good on Wednesday so having you to stay will help take her mind off it."

"Have you done anything about replacing Delphine?" his mother asked. At his silence, she sighed.

"Oh Marcus, what are you going to do with Megan when you have to be at work?"

"I hadn't thought about it."

"No, I don't imagine you have. Suppose I help you look for one while I'm there? I'd like to know that someone nice is looking after her, someone Megan likes and trusts."

"Okay," Marcus agreed. "That would be great. Let me know what flight you're getting, and I'll arrange for you to be picked up at the airport and taken to mine."

"I will do. Tell Megan her Grandma is looking forward to seeing her and sends her lots of love."

"I will, oh, and Mum…"

"Yes?"

"Thank you."

~Chapter Fourteen~
"I don't know how I'd manage without you."

Delphine's last few days sped past and then it was Wednesday afternoon, time for her to leave for good. Marcus had hoped the New York detective and the police artist would come whilst Delphine was still there.

Selfishly, he wanted Delphine's help with what was bound to be an unpleasant and stressful situation.

But the inspector had called saying he had pressing matters to attend to before he came. They would arrive Saturday and would like to speak to Megan over the weekend.

Marcus got the distinct feeling that the case had slipped in importance in the Inspector's eyes.

Perhaps it was the hopelessness of ever catching the attacker that had put the note of despondency in the Inspector's voice.

Now it was time to say goodbye to Delphine and Marcus knew it was going to be hard. They had both come to depend so much on her sweet nature and kindly ways.

He and Megan sat in the lounge deliberately not looking at each other whilst Delphine finished packing, double-checking in drawers and cupboards that nothing had been left behind because she was never coming back.

Her mobile rang and he heard her answer in English, then switch to French, her voice welcoming and happy.

There was a long silence, then he heard a rapid stream of French words that sounded questioning, almost disbelieving.

Trying not to listen, Marcus still couldn't help but hear the despair in her voice as she murmured some words in parting down the phone.

There was silence, a sigh, then the sound of a cupboard door being shut none too gently.

"Everything okay?" he asked as she appeared in the doorway.

"No," she huffed in impatience. "That was my best friend. Her little girl was going to be my bridesmaid, my only bridesmaid. But this morning my friend is telling me she has come down with chickenpox. She is very contagious, so cannot come. Neither of them can come."

"Oh no," he sympathised. "That's terrible, what will you do?"

Delphine glanced at Megan, then back at him.

"I know this is short notice, but I was wondering if you could both come to the wedding and if Megan could be my bridesmaid instead?"

Marcus stared at her in surprise as Megan's face lit up and she launched herself into Delphine's arms, nodding her head with delight.

"Yes," she cried happily, then turned to look at Marcus.

"Me?" she questioned.

In the face of such obvious enthusiasm, Marcus didn't want to be the killjoy but felt various points had to be raised.

"Will the dress fit Megan?"

"Oh yes."

Delphine ran a critical eye over Megan.

"The girls are almost the same size, if anything it may be a tiny bit too big, but that is nothing. It is a beautiful dress," she promised Megan. "With pink ballet slippers to wear with it."

"We'd have to try and get tickets for Eurostar."

"Pah, no problem, there are always spare seats, and when Jean picks me up from the station, he can pick you up as well."

"But what about accommodation? Where would we stay?"

"My friend had a twin-bedded room booked at the chateau. You can have that."

One by one she demolished his objections until Marcus raised his hands in acceptance, and Megan ran to throw herself into his arms.

"Me, me," she cried. "Me going to be a bridesmaid."

"Yes, it looks like you're going to be," he laughed, happy that she was happy, and the thought of a few days away raising his spirits enormously.

"Come, Megan." Delphine reached out a hand. "We must pack for you. You will need a change of clothes for the day after the wedding and night things. Come, let us go and pack."

They left the room.

Thinking rapidly, Marcus dialled Sally's mobile.

"Yes?"

"I need two tickets for me and Megan for Eurostar this afternoon."

"Right. Coming back?"

"Friday sometime, so reschedule any meetings I might have."

"Of course."

"My mother is arriving at Heathrow tomorrow evening, so I'll text you her flight details. Please arrange for someone to pick her up and take her to my apartment. I'll let her know we won't be back until the next day."

"I'll see if your mother would like to dine out, or if she'd prefer to have something delivered?"

"Yes, please, thank you, Sally."

"No problem."

"Can you arrange flowers for the apartment?"

"Already thought of it. If you approve, I'll order an arrangement of gardenias; they're your mother's favourites."

"Are they? Oh, right, get some of them then."

"Of course."

"Oh, and I know my mother wants to start looking for a new nanny, so perhaps you could look up agency details."

"Already have, the list is on your desk, and I will make sure your mother has a copy. I take it you're going to Delphine's wedding?"

"Yes."

"Good. Your gift was delivered to her parents' house last week. In case you're wondering, you bought the couple the coffee maker from their list."

"I like coffee," Marcus murmured.

"I know," replied Sally, crisply. "It seemed appropriate."

"Thank you, Sally. I don't know how I'd manage without you."

"You're very welcome," she said, sounding pleased.

"I'll see about getting the tickets and will forward them to your phone. Have a wonderful time, and I'll see you when you get back."

Safely settled on the train, Sally having secured them seats in the same compartment as Delphine, Marcus leant back against the softly padded headrest and closed his eyes, the bustle of the train's departure washing over him as white noise.

Suddenly incredibly weary, he hoped the room at the chateau was comfortable and wondered how long it would take to get there.

Most of all, he wondered what it would be like sharing a room with Megan.

"Shall I take Megan to get some supper?"

He opened his eyes. Delphine was standing in the aisle, one brow raised enquiringly.

"Yes." He fumbled in his wallet for money. "Get her whatever she wants, and something for yourself."

"Can we bring you something back?"

"Just coffee, thanks."

"Oui, come along Megan. Hold my hand and we'll see what nice things there are to eat in the buffet?"

Marcus watched them go, Megan confidently holding Delphine's hand, Brewster clutched to her chest, her head turning from side to side as she looked at all the people they passed.

Remembering that they had arranged to go and see the Lovejoys again that evening, Marcus dialled the house, surprised that he didn't need to look the number up, that he knew it by heart.

"Hello?"

"Finley?"

"No, it's Connor."

Oh, right, Connor. Hi, it's Marcus, is your mum there?"

"Mum!"

Wincing away from the ear-splitting yell, Marcus waited patiently.

"Hello?"

She was there, her voice merry and enquiring, no lingering memory in her voice of that kiss, that there had ever been any hint of anything other than friendship between them.

Marcus wondered if he had imagined it, knew he hadn't, but that he had to respect her wishes in this matter.

"Hi, it's me," he said.

"I know."

"Yes, of course, you do. Look, I'm sorry, but we can't come over tonight."

"Okay, no problem."

"We wanted to."

He hurried to reassure, for some reason it being vitally important to him that she knew just how much he wanted to.

"But, well, we're on our way to France. It was a last-minute decision."

"Are you going to Delphine's wedding?"

"Yes."

"The break will do you both the world of good."

"Delphine has asked Megan to be a last-minute, stand-in bridesmaid."

"Oh, how lovely. I bet Megan's so pleased about that."

"She is."

"She'll make a lovely bridesmaid. Make sure you take lots of pictures."

"I will."

"Good."

The silence stretched between them down the line.

"So," said Grace eventually. "I guess, perhaps, we'll see you when you get back."

"Yes, maybe, it'll be quite busy this weekend. The inspector in charge of the case is coming over with a police artist."

"Oh, I see."

Marcus heard from her voice that she did see all too well.

"Good luck with that, I hope it's not too stressful for Megan, or you."

"Thank you," he replied. "Oh, and my mother's over for a visit as well."

Grace laughed. "Well, good luck with that as well, and I hope that's not too stressful either."

"Probably will be," he said glumly.

She laughed again.

Silence again.

"Grace?"

"Yes, Marcus?"

She was no longer laughing now.

Her voice was soft and low.

"Grace, I ... Oh, nothing ... I'll call you when we get back."

"Okay."

He broke the connection.

She was gone.

Grace listened to the voice of the phone for a few moments, knowing he was gone, but still, listening...

Stupid woman, she told herself briskly and hung up. You stupid, stupid woman, what have you gone and done now...?

~Chapter Fifteen~
"No, no, no. Won't!"

By the time they finally reached the chateau it was almost midnight, and Megan was sound asleep. They had been collected at the train station in Paris by Jean, Delphine's handsome, good-natured fiancé, and Marcus held Megan as she slept all through the long car journey to the chateau.

Listening to Delphine and Jean softly chatting in French in the front seat, Marcus wished he had his brother, Luke's, aptitude with languages.

Drifting off himself, Marcus jolted awake when the car stopped, and Delphine shook him gently by the shoulder.

"Marcus," she whispered. "We're here."

Blinking stupidly, he grunted an affirmative and gently eased Megan down on the seat. Clambering from the car, he stretched his body, cramped from long hours of sitting and the weight of a little girl.

Jean took their luggage from the boot. "I will carry these," he said, in his heavily accented English. "You take the little girl."

Nodding, Marcus carefully slid Megan across the seat and into his arms. Mumbling, she turned into his chest, snuggling deeper.

Going into the beautifully elegant reception hall, Delphine explained the situation to the desk clerk, who shrugged and handed her a key.

"It's upstairs," she told him, and led the way up the grand flight of stairs, Jean following behind, loaded down with bags. A short walk along a plush carpeted corridor and then she was opening the door to a charming, twin-bedded room, elegant in the way only the French can manage.

"If you put her on the bed," she whispered. "I'll get her into it. I think we won't worry about teeth and face tonight. She's so tired, and it's a long day tomorrow."

Marcus nodded his agreement and gently eased Megan down onto the bed nearest the door. Taking the bags from Jean with a smile of thanks, he placed Megan's little unicorn backpack on the floor near her bed. Jean murmured something to Delphine in French and silently left the room.

Taking his bag into the bathroom, Marcus unpacked and put his and Megan's toiletries on the side near the sink.

Catching a glimpse of himself in the mirror, he was shocked at how tired and dispirited he looked. Maybe the last few months had taken more of a toll on him than he thought.

Leaving the bathroom, he found Delphine tucking the covers around Megan and giving her a gentle kiss on the forehead. She folded her clothes onto a chair and smiled at Marcus.

"I hope you will both sleep well, and I'll be along tomorrow at about eleven-thirty with Megan's dress."

"Thank you, Delphine, for everything."

"You're welcome. Good night, Marcus."

"Good night, Delphine."

After she had gone and no longer feeling sleepy, Marcus poured himself a whisky from the minibar and slouched into the chair by the window, listening to the silence, the only sound Megan's soft, even breaths.

Looking out into the darkness of the French countryside illuminated only by the slice of a silvery, crescent moon, he found himself thinking of Marla.

There had been no contact between them since the make-up incident. Marcus was surprised at how indifferent he was to that fact.

He was further surprised that he was having trouble remembering her face, the sound of her voice, the way she smiled – had she ever smiled?

In the months he knew her, Marcus doubted she ever had, not a truly sincere smile anyway.

Unbidden, an image of Grace arose in his mind, smiling at him across her old kitchen table, candlelight casting warming shadows over her features.

He remembered that last evening they had spent together after all the kids had gone to bed, that moment between them, the kiss that had felt like so much more. Or was he merely imagining it because he wanted it to be true?

Shaking his head in self-disgust, Marcus drained his glass and went to bed...

Awakening from a deep sleep at seven, Marcus stretched in his bed and looked across to find Megan awake, watching him.

"Good morning, Megan," he said, smiling as she squirmed about in her bed, kicking her legs with joy. "Did you sleep well? I know I did. My bed was very comfortable. Was yours comfy?"

There was a moment's silence as if Megan were considering his question.

"Yes," she replied carefully and grinned at him. "Me bridesmaid today."

"Yes, you are," he agreed. "But it's better to say, I am going to be a bridesmaid today. Can you say that Megan?"

"Yes."

"Will you?"

"No." She chortled out loud at the expression on his face.

"Monkey," he responded.

Giggling wildly, she rolled about in the bed making chimpanzee noises. Sitting bolt upright, she stared at him and announced.

"I am going to be a bridesmaid today."

Marcus felt the grin spread across his face. "Yes, you are," he agreed. "And a very pretty one, too."

Going down to breakfast, Marcus was surprised at how ravenous he was, though was it any wonder after having eaten nothing since yesterday morning.

Piling his plate with the French version of a full English, he sipped appreciatively at the excellent coffee as Megan crumbled a croissant all over her plate. Excitement at the day to come, completely taking away her appetite.

"Not hungry, honey?" he finally asked, and she shook her head sadly, surveying the mess on her plate.

"Never mind. Wipe your sticky fingers and drink your juice, there'll be plenty of food later.

With time to kill after breakfast, they wandered about the beautiful grounds of the chateau.

Discovering a delightful little folly that piqued Megan's interest, Marcus took pictures on his phone and listened to her humming a little tune as she played house in the miniature chateau.

Waving back as she posed gleefully in the windows, Marcus felt himself begin to relax. Grace had been right; the break was doing them good.

Grace.

There she was again. In his head and his thoughts. Why? What was it about her? Not beautiful, not by a long shot, certainly not compared to Marla or any of the other stunningly beautiful women he had dated in the past.

She was pretty, yes, but in a natural, off-handed sort of way, as if she were too busy and too concerned with other things to give a damn about her looks, or what other people thought of them.

Coming to a lake at the end of a long avenue of trees they found swans swimming in perfect harmony, and a bench perfectly positioned to sit on and watch.

"Pretty," said Megan, waving at them.

"Yes," he agreed. "They are pretty," and again, he thought of Grace.

Dressed in all her finery by a glowingly radiant Delphine, the image was spoilt by the glower of fiercely determined anger on Megan's face.

"Won't," she declared and stamped her ballet slipper clad foot on the bedroom floor.

"But Megan, sweetheart..."

"No, no, no. Won't!"

Delphine sighed in despair, looked over her shoulder at Marcus.

"Megan, honey, all Delphine is saying is that Brewster is a little too big to carry down the aisle. After all, you have that beautiful basket of flowers to carry. You can't manage both."

"Can. Brewster can sit in the basket."

"He's too big," snapped Delphine.

Marcus heard her reach the edge of her patience and marvelled that she hadn't reached it before. Then he was struck by a sudden brainwave.

"What about Mini Brew?" he asked.

Delphine raised her brows, and Megan's pout eased down a fraction.

"Look," he said, warming to his solution. "Mini Brew is tiny so he can sit in the middle of the flower basket quite easily. He can sort of represent Brewster. He'll be there to be your friend if you get nervous, but he won't spoil the flower arrangement or look silly on Delphine's extra special day,"

There was a silence as Megan looked at the tiny dog dangling from Brewster's collar, then glanced at Delphine. Perhaps she realised that she had pushed the bride-to-be a little too far, because slowly and reluctantly, Megan nodded.

"Wonderful," Delphine clapped her hands in relief and reached to unclip Mini Brew from Brewster's collar.

"We'll tuck him into the flowers, and no one will see him. He'll be hiding in there. A secret doggie only us three know about."

"But what about Brewster?" Megan demanded, and Marcus saw her lip begin to pout again.

"Well, he'll be waiting here for you…" began Delphine, but Marcus knew by the steely battle look on Megan's face that that solution was not acceptable.

"He can come to the wedding with me," he quickly broke in. "He can sit on my lap and watch you walk down the aisle. He'll keep me company while you're busy being bridesmaid and will be there waiting for you when the photos are all done."

There was another silence as Megan considered the plan from every angle, then held Brewster out to him and Marcus knew that he had won, that a compromise had been reached.

If anyone had told him three short months ago that he would be sitting at a wedding dressed in his favourite suit, alone – apart from a tatty, much chewed stuffed dog sitting proudly on his lap – he would have thought they were mad. Yet here he was, aware of the curiously amused glances and not caring.

His heart burst with pride as the music swelled and Delphine gracefully swept down the aisle on the arm of her doting papa, followed by Megan.

Her face solemn with the importance of the moment and her role as the only bridesmaid, she allowed herself a quick, sideways peek at him, a smile dimpling her face when she saw him. The smile deepened as he waved Brewster's paw at her.

Watching his little daughter be a bridesmaid for the first time Marcus felt absurdly moved, almost to tears, and realised he could not have been any prouder if she was his real daughter.

The congregation settled and the wedding ceremony began. Feeling the sentiment behind the words even if he didn't understand them, a pang of longing pierced his heart at the look Delphine and Jean exchanged with their rings.

Quickly looking at Megan's upright back, he watched her for the rest of the ceremony, amazed and impressed at her self-control.

Not allowing herself a single fidget or twitch, Megan remained bolt upright, both feet planted firmly on the ground, face forward, giving the occasion every ounce of her concentration.

It was an elegantly beautiful wedding, simple yet stunning in its classic execution, and Marcus and Megan – no longer nervous as her duties were over – thoroughly enjoyed the very tasty lunch provided for the guests.

Afterwards, there was music and dancing, and once night had draped itself over the chateau, most of the guests moved outside to watch the magnificent fireworks show.

Then a traditional send-off saw the bride and groom away on their honeymoon, with all the guests forming a processional arch for them to run under whilst being showered with confetti, rose petals, kisses, and best wishes.

At this point, feeling Megan getting sleepy and heavy on his shoulder, Marcus decided it was time for bed.

Carefully carrying her up the stairs, he returned good night wishes to a few of the other guests and let them into their room.

In their absence, the beds had been remade and turned down and the lamps switched on, so the room was warm and inviting.

Removing the chocolates from the pillows, Marcus slipped them into Megan's backpack for her to find the next day and set about easing her out of her bridesmaid finery.

Again, deciding to dispense with the usual teeth and face cleaning routine, he gently tucked her into bed where she was asleep in seconds.

Removing his tie and slipping off his shoes and jacket, Marcus poured himself another whisky and again settled in the same chair by the window.

Thinking about the day, he heard the soft strains of the wedding band seeping into the room through the slightly open window.

He thought of the journey home tomorrow and sighed. Then he thought about his mother's visit and sighed again.

Checking the time on his phone he saw it was gone midnight. She would be there by now, in his apartment, probably asleep, tired from the flight.

His phone vibrated in his hand. Surprised, he checked the caller ID. Surprise turned to concern, and he quickly slipped into the bathroom, closing the door firmly behind him so as not to awaken Megan.

"Sally?"

"I'm sorry, Marcus, so sorry to call you at this hour, but I thought I'd better let you know immediately."

"Know? Know what? Sally, what's happened?"

Concern sharpening his voice, Marcus's imagination was running wild exploring every awful scenario.

"It's your apartment, Marcus, it's on fire!"

~Chapter Sixteen~
"I think Grace may be in trouble,"

Marcus gaped, speechless with shock. Hearing Sally's concerned 'Hello? Hello?' down the line, he pulled himself back together.

"On fire? What? Sally, how, what?"

"I'm standing outside it now. The fire brigade is here, and they think they can contain it to your apartment, but they've evacuated the other residents just in case. It's chaos here, people in dressing gowns all milling about."

"My mother! She's in there, Sally!"

"No, no, it's all right, Marcus, she's not." Sally hurried to reassure. "Her flight was cancelled due to technical problems with the plane, and it's been rescheduled for tomorrow morning,"

"Thank God," he gasped, his brain struggling to catch up. "Do they know how it started?"

"No, as I said, it's chaos here."

"Why are you there, Sally? It's gone eleven."

"They called me. When they couldn't get hold of you, they called me. I'm the second contact with the concierge for your apartment."

Glancing at his phone, Marcus saw a call had come through to him an hour earlier, but he hadn't heard it over the music, so it had gone to voicemail. "I'm sorry you were bothered, Sally."

"No, that's fine, Marcus. I'm so sorry, it looks like it's all gone, everything." His unflappable PA's voice quivered, and he tried to comfort her.

"It's okay, Sally, it's only stuff. It can be replaced. We weren't in there, neither was Mum."

"Yes, thank heavens you went to France when you did. If you'd been in there ... Marcus, it took hold so quickly you would both probably have been killed. Just thinking about it, I..."

"But we weren't. We're okay. Now I want you to go home, Sally. There's nothing more you can do tonight. Go home. We'll sort it tomorrow."

"But ... perhaps I should..."

"Go home, Sally. Thank you for everything, but you need to go home now."

There was silence, then she sighed. "All right, I'll go home, but I'll get onto the insurance company first thing tomorrow. Do you want me to book you both into a hotel?"

"No, I'll call Luke in the morning. They're back from their holiday. We'll crash with them until we sort something out."

"Right, yes, of course ... do you want me to...?"

"I want you to go home and get some sleep."

"Okay, I will, and Marcus, I am so sorry."

The next morning when she awoke, Marcus gently told Megan the news. How there had been a fire but she wasn't to worry as no one had been hurt, and that they couldn't go back to the apartment because it was all dirty and wet from the firemen's hoses.

Eyes wide, Megan asked a few questions, more concerned about where they were to sleep that night rather than anything else. Relieved at being told they would stay with Luke, Arianna, and

Lucia until they found somewhere else to live, she fell into a tired silence for all the drive to Paris, and much of the train journey home.

It wasn't until they emerged from the Channel Tunnel and the green countryside of the county of Kent began to flash past the windows, that she tugged on his sleeve. "Uncle Marcus?"

"Yes, Megan?"

"We need a new home now, don't we?"

"Yes, that's right, we do."

"Well, if we need a new home and the Lovejoys have to sell theirs, why don't we buy it off them?"

Stunned by the childish logic, Marcus stared at her in silence for a while.

"It's an awfully big house, Megan," he tried to carefully explain. "Far too big for just us."

"There's only four Lovejoys," Megan reasoned. "And there'll be three of us once we find me a new nanny, that's only one less. And Grandma will come and stay lots of times, so we'll need space for her." Her expression turned to wheedling.

"And when I start school, I'll want lots of room for my friends to stay, and maybe the rest of the family can come sometimes. Uncle Liam, when he's back from war, and Auntie Kit, when she's not singing all over the world. And we could have big parties, and everyone could stay."

Drawn into the wonderful fairy tale she was spinning, Marcus was silent, thinking about it.

"It's just, if the Lovejoys can't live in their house anymore," she explained, "I don't want anybody else to live there except, maybe, us."

And Marcus realised she was absolutely, completely right. No one else *could* live in that house. No one else *should* be allowed to live in that house, except the Lovejoys – and maybe him and Megan. Pulling out his phone he dialled, his eyes never leaving Megan's hopeful face.

"Sally."

"Yes?"

"Please call the estate agent and make an offer for the Lovejoys' house."

"For how much?"

"Full asking price."

"But Marcus, don't you think you should offer lower? We both know they'll take whatever they can get."

"I said full asking price."

"Very well, I'll call them now."

"Thank you, Sally. We'll go straight to Luke's from the station. Did you have new clothes for us sent there?"

"Yes, the driver took them around earlier."

"Thank you," he said. "Have you heard from my mother again?"

"Yes, she said she'll call you later, but for now she'll stay in New York."

"Good, it's probably for the best."

"Probably, oh, and Marcus ..." But he had already hung up, staring at Megan, their eyes serious with the enormity of their decision.

A smile spread across Megan's face. "The house is going to be ours," she whispered.

"Yes," he agreed. "It is." An answering smile crept across his face as the consequences of his actions dawned on him. "It's going to be ours."

"How much damage is there?" Luke handed his brother a coffee and settled in the armchair opposite, his eyes serious and concerned.

"Enough," Marcus sighed. "The apartment is trashed and everything that was in it was either burnt or ruined by the water. The insurance company are having a field day. They've already got fire experts crawling all over it."

"Why?" There was a sharp note of interest in Luke's voice. "Do they think it was arson?"

"No, of course not!" Shocked, Marcus stared at his brother. "Why, what are you suggesting?"

"Nothing," Luke hesitated. "But again, it's a little too coincidental. Megan starts talking and a few days later your apartment catches fire. It's only the fact you decided to go away at the last minute that saved you both." He paused, considering Marcus's dazed expression.

"Oh, forget it. It's me being suspicious as usual, Arianna's always accusing me of being a cynic. Maybe she's right."

"You can't possibly believe the fire has any connection to Monica's death, do you?"

"No, of course not, it's … well, it's like I said, I don't like coincidences."

"It couldn't be anything other than an accident." Marcus stopped, hearing the uncertainty in his voice. The two men considered each other in silence, their blue eyes thoughtful.

"Probably best we don't share your theory with anyone yet …" Marcus murmured, and Luke nodded in agreement.

"I'm probably wrong anyway, I usually am about most things, according to both my wife and my daughter."

"When did you know?" Marcus asked.

"Know what?"

"That Lucia was your daughter, even though she wasn't really yours."

Luke thought for a moment. "I think," he began slowly, "it was on the plane after we had rescued her and were flying back. She fell asleep and I tucked a blanket around her. I think it was at that point I realised I loved her as much as I loved Arianna, that they were a package deal. Love one, love the other."

Marcus nodded, thinking of Megan, and of how much her small hand was already clenched tightly around his heart.

"So," continued Luke. "When is she being interviewed by the police?"

"It's been put off again," Marcus replied. "There is some big case breaking over there and the inspector couldn't spare the time to fly over. He apologised and said it'll be next week sometime, maybe."

Again, the men exchanged glances.

"Sounds to me," said Luke, "as if they've given up even looking for the man responsible."

"I think so too," agreed Marcus.

Both looked up as Arianna entered the room, stunningly beautiful in a green silk gown, Lucia and Megan trailing in her wake, one clutching a pair of dark green, high heeled evening sandals, the other a matching green evening bag.

"Hey, gorgeous," whistled Marcus, and Arianna flushed with pleasure. Sitting on a chair she held out a hand and Megan handed her the shoes, which Arianna slipped onto her small feet.

"Are you sure you wouldn't like us to cancel?" she fussed. "We could easily, then we could stay home tonight with you and Megan?"

"Don't you dare," laughed Marcus. "You go. Your first anniversary – that's something special. What are you celebrating? I know it's not your wedding anniversary because that's April."

Luke and Arianna exchanged glances, and the flush on his sister-in-law's cheeks deepened as his brother's eyes twinkled with the memory.

"Oh, I see," he drawled. "It's *that* anniversary, is it?" and laughed at Arianna's embarrassment.

"We can't even leave Lucia to keep you company," commented Luke, standing up and pulling on his suit jacket.

"She's going to Isabella's, and I know they've got a whole evening planned, although …" He glanced out of the window at the weather. "I think the outdoor bit will have to be abandoned, it's looking a bit wild out there."

Marcus followed his glance. Since arriving earlier that day the weather had progressively worsened, with winds gusting fiercely, and storm clouds being tossed about a darkening sky.

"Don't worry about us," he reassured. "We have somewhere we can maybe go."

Megan's face lit up in an enthusiastic beam, and she jumped excitedly from foot to foot.

"The Lovejoys? Oh, please, yes."

"Well, I'll call them," he said. "But they might not be in, or it might not be convenient for us to go around tonight."

"They'll be in," insisted Megan. "Where else would they be? And of course, it will be all right, why wouldn't it be?"

And Marcus had to agree. The thought of the Lovejoy's being anywhere but in their home was unthinkable. Likewise, was the thought of them being anything but welcoming.

Hustling Lucia into a coat, Luke and Arianna left a few minutes later after checking they had keys. Reassuring them that if they didn't go to the Lovejoys, there was plenty of food in the fridge and that they were to help themselves.

Reassuring, assuring, pacifying, and agreeing, Marcus and Megan waved them out into the wild night, struggling to close the front door against the force of the wind, feeling the storm in the air and the threat of rain it carried.

"Now call them," ordered Megan.

Dialling the number, he waited.

"Hello?"

"Grace?"

"No, it's Zoey."

"Is your mum there?"

"No, Marcus, she's not here…"

Marcus frowned, hearing the worry in Zoey's voice. "Zoey, what is it? Where is she?"

"She went to the allotment because she's worried about the crops. She wouldn't let us go with her. She said we had to stay here because of the weather. So, she's there all alone, Marcus, and I'm worried." He heard her take a deep, shuddering breath down the line.

"The radio says it's only going to get worse this evening and there's so much to harvest. She can't do it all alone, but she told me to stay here with the boys, and … I'm worried, Marcus."

"We're on our way, Zoey. Hold tight, we'll sort something out when we get there."

"Oh, but I didn't mean…"

"We're on our way. We'll be there as quickly as possible." Marcus hung up and looked at Megan.

"I think Grace may be in trouble," he said.

"Then we must help her," Megan replied.

"Yes," he agreed. "We will, but there's something we have to do on the way."

~Chapter Seventeen~
"Zoey said you might need some help."

If Grace was the sort of woman who cried, she'd be crying right about now. But she wasn't. So instead, she screamed her fury to the skies, her yells lost in the ever-increasing, gusting wind. The allotment was deserted, all the others had given up and gone home long ago.

"Go home, Grace." Ted, the owner of Maisie the goat had urged her. "It's too dangerous to stay here, go home."

But she couldn't. They were her crops, her way of feeding her family for the following year. If she left them for the storm to destroy, they'd have nothing.

Maybe not. The estate agent had phoned that morning with avaricious delight in her voice. Mr Blackwood had come back with an offer for the full asking price. He wasn't in a chain and was a cash buyer; it couldn't be better.

The agent strongly advised she accept his offer. After all, she wouldn't get a better one.

Grace knew she wouldn't get a better offer. She wasn't stupid; she knew the house was overpriced. That even though it was a great, big, wonderful house, simply oozing with charm, it needed so much work it would cost the buyer many thousands more simply to do the basics.

But she stalled, told the disbelieving agent she would think about it and heard the barely concealed scorn in the woman's voice when she advised her not to think about it for too long.

Buyers like Mr Blackwood didn't come along that often and were to be snapped up when they did.

Mr Blackwood.

He's not Mr Blackwood, she wanted to scream at the woman. He's Marcus. Tall, gorgeous, kind, surprisingly wonderful Marcus. Not simply the suit she had initially dismissed him as.

He was more.

Oh, so much more.

Thinking about him ... about the way he was with Megan, the way he had turned his life around and accepted without a murmur the responsibility unexpectedly dumped on him of his sister's orphaned child, giving Megan all the support and love she needed without ever once complaining.

Grace could love him for that alone.

But then there was the way he was with her kids. Kind and considerate with Zoey. Gentle but firm with the boys.

He didn't see it; didn't realise that they were different around him, but she did. They were so desperate to please him, to impress him.

They straightened up whenever he was around, seeking his approval, trying so hard to make him see and be proud of them that her heart ached for her poor, fatherless boys.

And then there was the way he was with her.

Don't go there, her head ordered. But I want to, pouted her heart, and go there it did.

All those looks, those moments. Those times when he looked at her, really looked at her, and she knew he was seeing the real her. Was seeing past the dreadlocks, the nose piercing – the hippie clothes she had hidden behind ever since Daniel died.

He *saw* her. He looked right into her. Sometimes she felt he knew her better than anyone. Maybe better than Zoey did.

And then there had been that kiss.

Oh, that kiss.

She could pretend all she liked to him, act all casual, all "oh, it didn't matter, it was only a kiss", but she couldn't fool herself.

It did matter, and it hadn't only been a kiss.

Alone for so long, untouched since Daniel, it had been the shock of attraction that had made her nearly yield to him.

If the milk hadn't boiled over, she'd have gone to bed with him, would have dragged him up the stairs to her room. Desperate to hold him, to lie in his arms and feel like a woman again.

Thank heavens the milk boiled over then, said her head. Yeah right, drawled her heart.

And now he had made an offer for her house, and she felt sure he was doing it for her because he knew she needed the money, and he was rich, so very, very rich, so why not? Give the hippie chick what she wanted, pay her off.

No, she was being unfair, both her head and her heart agreed on this. Marcus wasn't like that.

Oh, he might have been, once.

But Megan had changed him. The house and the kids had changed him.

Grace herself had changed him. Made him softer, gentler. Made him a better man.

Presumptuous much scoffed her head. You, change him? As if. But she had, she knew she had. She had seen the change in him.

From the stuffed shirt who came to view the house, to the man who kissed her so thoroughly and completely in her kitchen, there was a world of difference.

So why wasn't she jumping for joy about the news he had made an offer on the house?

Sorrow at leaving her home.

Maybe.

Apprehension at what the future held for her and the kids?

Probably.

Despair that once they sold him the house, she'd never see him again.

Definitely.

The wind gusted, and Grace gripped the basket she was holding. The peas had all been picked and were safely stowed away in the shed, now she was stripping the runner bean plants of their load.

Trying to harvest those crops most vulnerable to high winds first, she allowed herself a moment to think of all she still had to do and groaned with despair.

This was no job for one small woman.

Usually, she had Zoey and the boys to help. Sometimes she even laboured for fellow allotment keepers in exchange for their help with her harvest.

But now she was all alone, under a sky the colour of an old bruise, her face being buffeted by the fierce, stinging wind, her eyes constantly attacked by particles being viciously blown into them by the gale.

It had been too dangerous to bring the kids along, and besides, Finley had gone down with a nasty cold a few days earlier, complete with a cough that seemed to rip his lungs apart and left him weak and wheezing. There was no way he could have come, and no way he could have been left alone.

So instead, she was alone.

Under an angry sky, with a storm rapidly upgrading itself into as close as England could get to a hurricane.

She was scared.

There, she admitted it.

For almost the first time in her life, she, Grace Lovejoy, was properly scared. It frightened her, the savagery of the elements, the fact she knew it was going to beat her.

It was getting worse, the gusting winds taking on aspects of a gale, and she knew she was fighting a losing battle. She would never get her crops in before the threatened storm broke directly overhead.

Finally finished picking the runner beans, she staggered over into the shed and emptied the basket into the large storage bin at the back. No time to sort or arrange nicely.

Tomorrow, once the storm had died down, they would all come back with the boys' old go-cart, load everything on, and trundle it all home. There, it could be sorted, graded, washed, prepped, and stored.

Leaving the shed, the door was practically ripped from her hands, and she fought with it for several long, painful moments before she managed to latch it securely.

Turning, she surveyed her plot again, wiping a shaking hand over eyes stung to tears by the wind.

Right, now the potatoes. A high-value crop, the family relied on a good harvest to provide the bulk of their meals. Bracing herself, she got another bucket and grabbed her fork.

Car lights cut across her plot. In the deepening gloom of the afternoon, she leant on her fork and watched as the long, sleek Jaguar reversed onto her plot. Carefully parking on the grass verge, the lights went out and the driver's side door opened.

Recognising the car, her heart stopped then clenched tightly in acknowledgement.

It was Marcus.

He clambered from the car, looked around and saw her, holding up a hand in greeting. She frowned, there was something different about him.

Then she realised he was in jeans, not a suit. Jeans so new she could see the sharp, pressed creases running horizontally across his legs where he must have just removed them from their packaging.

The thick knit, chunky sweater he was wearing looked new too, as did the waterproof coat he was carrying over one arm.

Going to the boot of the car, he opened it and sat on the edge. Reaching in, he removed a pair of Wellington boots so new they shone.

Carefully, he unlaced his smart leather shoes and tossed them into the boot behind him, then pulled on the Wellies.

Standing up, he stamped into them, easing his feet around in unfamiliar footwear.

Finally, he reached into the boot and pulled out a brand-new garden fork, ripped the tag off it, and dropped that into the boot before slamming down the lid and turning to face her.

Uncertainly, clutching his fork like a weapon, he looked at her and their eyes met in the unnatural light of the early dusk.

Grace didn't think it would be possible to love anyone as much as she loved him at that precise moment.

He had come to help her.

Not only that, but he had also gone to the trouble to come prepared.

It was the most romantic thing anyone had ever done for her.

He tramped across the churned-up ground towards her. The wind ripped the words from his mouth, and she shook her head, laughing.

Cupping a hand to her ears, she had to wait until he was by her side before, she could hear him. Leaning down to her, he placed a hand on her shoulder and almost bellowed in her ear.

"Zoey said you might need some help."

She nodded, too relieved to even pretend not to be happy to see him.

"A little," she agreed.

He looked around the plot.

"What do you want me to do?" he asked.

She took him by the hand and drew him to the other end of the potato patch. She showed him how to carefully fork through the earth, how to get the prongs between the roots and lever up, revealing the fat, dirt-encrusted clumps. How to pull up the plant, shake it, then dump it in the bucket.

He nodded after one display, then pulled on and zipped up his jacket and set to the task without another word, leaving her to start the other end.

She looked back at him now and then, checking he was okay, seeing to her disbelief what a difference his superior strength made to getting the job done.

Freshly inspired, she set to with renewed vigour. Maybe there was hope after all.

~Chapter Eighteen~
"I think there's someone in the house,"

They laboured for what seemed hours, not stopping, and only talking when Marcus enquired as to the next task and Grace gave instructions. When it became too dark to see, Grace switched on the spotlight fastened to the front of the shed, deliberately angled to cast long, bright light over the whole plot.

The storm worsened, and still, they worked. All the potatoes were rescued, the carrots, beetroot, onions, leeks, and garlic.

Watching Marcus struggle with a couple of giant marrows, she laughed at him and was rewarded by his exasperated, little boy grin.

Finally, Grace pulled up the last of the spinach, threw it into a basket and headed for the shed. "That's it!" she yelled.

Marcus, on the other side of the plot, shook his head and held a hand to his ears. Giving up on trying to make herself heard, she merely waved him over and gestured to the shed.

Inside, the reprieve of being out of the driving winds was instant and welcome. Looking around at her harvest home, Grace wiped away tears of relief, turned to Marcus as he bundled through the door, pulling it firmly closed behind him.

"Thank you," she cried. "Thank you so much. I could never have done this without you. We managed to get it all in. I thought I was going to lose so much."

Marcus shrugged, looking pleased, and leaned his fork against the shed wall. Glancing around, he surveyed the fruits of their labour with satisfaction. "I'm glad we got it all in," he said, glancing at his hands and wincing.

Instant concern struck her. "Let me see!"

"It's nothing."

"Let me see," she ordered.

Reluctantly, he turned his hands over and let her see the red raw state of his palms. Unused to such hard, physical labour, they had quickly blistered. Determined not to stop, he ignored them until the blisters had split and oozed, shooting darts of agony through his hands every time he put pressure on them, yet still, he dug.

Partly mannish pride – not wanting to admit he was weaker than her – and partly willpower not to give in, driving him ever onwards.

Frowning, she examined his damaged hands.

"You should have said something," she muttered, angry that he was hurt. Angry at him for not saying something. Angry with herself for causing him pain.

"It's okay," he reassured her. "They don't hurt, much." Pursing her lips, she shot him a look.

"Don't go all macho on me," she warned, then reached for the small first aid tin she always kept on the shelf. Basic, it dealt with the various cuts, scrapes, bruises, and stings that the kids tended to end up with when working alongside her.

"Hold on," she murmured, ripping open an antiseptic wipe. "This will sting a bit."

"It's fine, I can ... bugger me, that hurt!" he yelped.

"Don't be such a baby," she teased him, softly smearing antiseptic cream over his poor hands, enjoying looking after him. She finished off with large plasters over the worst of the wounds.

"Leave them on for a day or so," she advised. "Then take them off so the skin can heal."

"Thank you," he said, surveying the plasters with almost pride. After all, they were very big plasters covering wounds gained helping a damsel in distress.

"I made an offer on the house," he said, without looking up.

"I know."

"You haven't accepted it yet."

"I know."

"Why?"

"I've been busy. I wanted to think about it."

"What's to think about? You need to sell, and I need a home. Now, more than ever."

"Why? Why now more than ever?"

"Because whilst we were in France, there was a fire. It destroyed my apartment. It's all gone, Grace, there's nothing left."

She gasped, staring at him in horror. "A fire?"

"Yes."

"Was anybody hurt?"

"No, they managed to contain it to my apartment. Although, it's a miracle Megan, and I weren't killed. If we hadn't made that last-minute decision to go to France, we'd have been there, asleep, and it spread so quickly. We probably wouldn't have had time to get out."

Grace took a shaky breath. "You were lucky, Marcus, so lucky. You could've both been killed."

"I know."

"But why my house? I thought you said it was too big for you. That it needed too much work?"

"It is, and it does, but Megan said, and I agreed with her, that we couldn't bear the thought of anyone else living in that house except the Lovejoys, apart from maybe – us."

She stared at him for the longest time, thinking about what he had said.

"I don't want to leave my home," she finally whispered. "But if I have to, if someone else has to live in it, someone other than us, then I guess I'd rather it was you and Megan."

"You could come back and visit anytime you wanted to," he assured.

"Yes," she agreed, although they both knew she was lying. Once they left, the Lovejoys could never come back, that it would kill them coming back when it no longer belonged to them.

Again, they stared at one another, until suddenly the mood changed.

Pupils dilated. Breath quickened.

Sensation prickled down their spines as arousal, sharp, and tinged with desperate need, welled in the space between them. Feeling it roil in her gut, she swallowed and licked her dry lips. His eyes were upon her, eating her up whole.

She wanted him, she knew it, accepted it.

Knew he wanted her back.

"Grace…"

He stepped closer and put a hand to her dreadlocks, not caring about the dirt smeared on her chin, only seeing the woman underneath.

"Don't speak," she ground out the words. "Don't speak, just do…"

He closed the gap between them, his hands on her arms yanking her close. Then he was holding her, his strong arms enfolding her close to his tall, firm body.

Groaning with relief, she lifted her head to his and allowed him to claim her mouth. No hesitation, no gentleness. This time the kiss was brutal, savage. It claimed and was claimed in return. Giving no quarter, taking no prisoners, it demanded, and it took.

Gripping her by the waist, he lifted and settled her onto the potting table. Hands shaking, he ripped at the zip of her coat, pushing it down over her shoulders, his hands cupping her breasts through her t-shirt.

Crying out in shock, she struggled with the new zip on his jacket. Finally yanking it down, she pulled him closer, plastering herself against him, wrapping her legs around him. Uncaring of the mud she smeared down his new jeans, she ground herself onto him.

Slipping his fingers under the edge of her t-shirt, he found her collarbone, the delicate sturdiness of it. Rubbing with his thumb, he deepened the kiss, consuming and devouring her. He pulled back, his fingers toying with the zip of her cargo pants.

"Grace?"

"Yes," she groaned, hands going down to help him. "Yes, now, please, oh yes..."

Given the red light, he began to ease it down, his gaze never leaving her flushed, expectant face. Need, hunger, want, desire – all for him – were etched onto her expression.

"Grace," he murmured, his voice husky. "I..."

But whatever he'd been about to say was drowned out by the insistent ringing of his phone. Cursing, he stopped, pulled back.

"Leave it," she gasped, desperate to have his hands on her again. "Just leave it."

He considered it, and he did try. Running his hands over her back, he tried to ignore it, but he couldn't. Too engrained a response, he stepped back from her and yanked the phone angrily from his pocket. Staring at the caller ID, he recognised the number.

"It's Zoey," he said.

Instantly, she was all concern, sliding down off the table. Her face a mask of enquiry, she waited impatiently as he answered the phone.

"Zoey, it's okay, we've nearly finished, we'll be home soon. How's Megan, is she …? What? Zoey? What's the matter?"

Beside him, he felt Grace stiffen in alarm, and he flicked the phone to loudspeaker.

"Zoey, love," she called anxiously. "What's wrong?"

"Mum." They both heard the edge of fear in her voice. "The lights have all gone out, but I don't think it's the storm. I can see lights on in the neighbour's house. It's only ours."

"It's an old fuse box, honey," Grace tried to reassure. "It might have tripped."

"I know," Zoey's reply was taut with apprehension. "But I don't think that's it…"

There was a pause, they heard her gasp and the sound of far-away breaking glass.

"Zoey!" Grace cried. "What is it? What's happened?"

"I think there's someone in the house," Zoey whispered, and then the line went dead.

~Chapter Nineteen~
"something bad is coming."

The day felt wrong. Zoey couldn't put her finger on why it felt wrong, it just did. She felt it first when tending her bees.

Normally placid, especially around her, she heard a new frantic tone in their buzzing and sensed a purpose in their frenzied to-ing and fro-ing to their hives.

"What is it?" she murmured. "What's wrong?"

Everyone laughed when she said her bees spoke to her, everyone but mum, that was. Mum smiled and nodded.

Everyone else thought she was joking or was saying it to be clever.

But it was true, they did.

Oh, not speak to her as in with words, that would be silly, but they communicated with her. She knew if they were happy, and all was right with the hive. She knew when they were stressed about anything, and she knew if extreme weather conditions were on their way by the change in the bees' flying patterns.

Today she sensed something bad, something big, was on its way and she glanced up nervously into the sky.

All day the winds had been increasing, gaining in strength, and now as she watched the boughs of the old oak tree thrash in a mighty gust of wind, Zoey could feel the gathering pressure in the air.

The radio had warned of strong, gusting winds heading their way, but she had a feeling it was going to be more, much more.

Peering through the veil of her old beekeeper's hat, she saw mum pacing down the garden towards her, anxiety evident in every taut line of her body.

"I'm going to the allotment. I'm worried about the crops. If this wind gets much worse, they'll be ripped out of the ground."

Pulling off the hat in concern, Zoey dropped it to the grass.

"I'll come with you," she said, but her mother shook her head firmly.

"No, you stay here with the kids. Finley's still got that nasty cold so he can't go, and I don't want him left alone. You stay with them. I'll go and harvest as much as I can before it gets too bad."

"Mum, no, I don't think you should go ... It's getting wild, and the radio said worse is to come."

"All the more reason for me to rescue as much as I can. We rely on those crops, Zoey, you know we do."

"I know, it's just ... I'm scared, Mum, something's not right, something bad is coming."

"Something bad? Zoey, whatever do you mean?"

"The bees told me, warned me, that something bad is about to happen. It could be the storm, but I don't know. I've never seen them like this before, so agitated, and nervous."

"It's just a storm, Zoey, and we've weathered plenty of those in our time, haven't we? Don't worry, I'll be careful, and if it gets too bad, I'll come home."

"Mum, please, I'm scared, please don't go."

Her mother frowned, put a hand to Zoey's face and felt her trembling.

"Zoey, this is so unlike you."

"I know, I … I can't explain it. It's like every nerve ending in my body is telling me we must leave, go, now. Grab the boys and run away."

"It's the storm," her mother reassured her.

"It's all that electricity in the air. Now I've got to go. I'll be back as soon as I can, but if I'm not back by suppertime make sure Finley eats something and make sure he keeps up with his fluids, oh, and takes his black pepper and honey tea for that cough."

Zoey managed a small smile.

"He hates that."

"I know, but it'll ease the congestion on his chest. There's a bit of chocolate in the cupboard. Tell him if he drinks it all without any fuss, he can have that."

Zoey nodded, watching as her mum zipped up her old combat jacket.

"Mum…"

"Yes?"

"Please, be careful…"

Trying to keep busy, to keep her mind off her sense of impending danger, Zoey read to the boys, played cards with them, then made Finley drink his tea, pacifying his groans with the chocolate, then pacifying Connor's cries of, "it's not fair" with promises of chocolate when/if he succumbed to Finley's cold.

Worry for mum etched its way deep into her mind until the boys picked up on it, whispering to each other every time her back was turned.

It was a relief when the phone rang.

Zoey snatched it up convinced it might be mum. Although how could it be when she didn't even have a mobile?

"Hello?"

"Grace?"

"No, it's Zoey."

"Is your mum there?"

"No, Marcus, she's not here..."

"Zoey, what is it? Where is she?"

"She went to the allotment because she's worried about the crops. She wouldn't let us go with her. She said we had to stay here because of the weather. So, she's there all alone, Marcus, and I'm worried."

She took a deep, shuddering breath.

"The radio says it's only going to get worse this evening and there's so much to harvest. She can't do it all alone, but she told me to stay here with the boys, and ... I'm worried, Marcus."

"We're on our way, Zoey. Hold tight, we'll sort something out when we get there."

"Oh, but I didn't mean..."

"We're on our way. We'll be there as quickly as possible."

Hanging up the phone, Zoey felt a profound sense of relief that Marcus was on his way. Maybe he would go in his car and get Mum, persuade her to come home.

Either way, his strong male presence was something she longed for more than anything.

Zoey liked Marcus.

She hadn't at first.

At first, she had been convinced he was nothing more than a rich idiot in a smart suit, but she soon saw through that when he laughed at the tomato incident and had teased the boys.

Then he brought Megan around.

Poor little Megan with the big eyes and the silence that spoke volumes. After they left, Mum took her to one side and told her what had happened.

Shocked, Zoey tried to imagine what Megan had gone through. The terror of the carjacking, watching as her mum and dad were shot in front of her.

The fear of thinking she was about to die, then the trauma of lying between their bodies on a dark country road all night, alone.

It didn't bear thinking about.

After the whole car cleaning trauma which had set Megan talking again, Zoey sensed a change in the relationship between Mum and Marcus. Previously relaxed and friendly, now there was a stiffness there.

A not spoken about or referred to tension between them, as if something had happened to change the way they viewed each other.

Zoey watched and wondered.

She liked Marcus, she did, but if he hurt Mum, he would have her to contend with.

Then today he made an offer on the house for the full asking price. Mum thought she didn't know, but Zoey did.

The estate agent had called back later to try to convince mum to accept it, but she had been out getting in the washing, so Zoey had taken the call.

Promising the rather strident woman that she would speak to mum about it and would urge her to accept, she didn't.

Instead, she had hugged the knowledge to herself and wondered some more.

Zoey didn't want to leave her home but was pragmatic enough to realise they had to. Had even accepted it, to a degree.

Had thought about how great it would be to have a shower that worked, to be able to afford a TV, a computer, and the internet, all the things her friends took for granted.

Thinking about it some more, she had even decided if anyone had to get their home then she didn't mind so much it being Marcus and Megan.

Because those guys belonged here too. The house had accepted them, and they needed a home, so why not?

And now they were coming over and Zoey was relieved. This all felt too much for her to handle. She wanted a grown-up here.

She wanted Marcus with his strong, calm manner to make everything right again.

"Marcus and Megan are on their way," she announced.

The boys visibly perked up.

"Cool, maybe Marcus will play Go Fish with us," said Connor.

It was possible to tell them apart now, well until Finley's cold cleared up it was.

"I don't think so," said Zoey, still clutching the phone. "I'm hoping he'll go and get Mum."

"Will they stay for supper?" asked Finley, his eyes lighting up at the thought of food.

Usually a bottomless pit, the cold had increased his appetite until Zoey seriously wondered where he put it all.

"Probably," she agreed and replaced the handset. "So why don't you guys help me get stuff ready."

When they finally got there half an hour later, Zoey was astounded to see Marcus in brand new jeans and realised she never thought of him in anything other than his crisp, expensive, perfectly tailored suits.

The jeans looked good on him she decided, made him seem more human, more approachable, not so perfect.

He hustled Megan into the warm, candle and lamp lit kitchen, and looked around.

"She not back yet?" obviously meaning Grace.

Zoey shook her head.

"No, there was so much to harvest, and you know Mum, she won't stop until she gets it all in ... or something happens to her."

Marcus looked at the gusting winds slapping against the windows, then met her gaze in a shared look of concern.

"I'll go and see if I can help or persuade her to come back. Megan honey, you stay here with Zoey and the boys. I'll be back soon."

"Yes," agreed Megan happily, and wandered over to watch the boys as they cheated at cards.

"I'll be as quick as I can," he reassured her in a low voice so as not to alarm the younger children. "And Zoey, don't worry. Your mum is tough, and she's not stupid. Once she sees it's getting worse, she'll give in and come home."

"Will she?" Zoey shook her head, fear again gripping her throat.

"I don't know, Marcus, I'm scared. Something doesn't feel right ... I can't explain it, but I've been feeling this way all day."

Marcus frowned, took a small pen and notepad from his pocket, and hastily jotted down a number. "Look, this is my mobile. Call me if you need me, or if I miss your mum, and she turns up here."

Zoey nodded, took the note, and tucked it under the telephone.

Once he was gone back out into the storm, she made a deliberate effort to pull herself together. Not wanting to infect the children with her fears, she smiled at them.

"Shall I make us some supper?" she asked calmly, and there was an eager round of agreement.

~Chapter Twenty~
"He'll have to catch me first,"

After supper had been eaten and cleared away, the boys wanted to carry on with their drawing. Their school was holding a drawing competition, and both were keen to enter.

Zoey suspected Finley's keenness was only due to wishing to be like Connor, as Connor was the artist in the family.

Megan watched with interest, her face lighting up when Zoey said, "Would you like to draw something, Megan?"

"Yes," agreed Megan, and eagerly accepted the drawing pad and pot of crayons.

Silence fell upon the kitchen.

Wandering to the window, Zoey peered out into the darkness, shivering at the dimly glimpsed branches that tossed wildly in the wind.

Feeling the chill seeping through the glass, she shivered and grasped the curtain ready to draw it and shut the night outside, when she stopped and frowned.

Had that been a figure?

There, over by the fence, a tall, human-shaped, figure. Zoey could have sworn she saw something, or someone, slip over the fence from next door into their garden.

Wishing for the first time they had normal outdoor electric lights like everyone else, Zoey watched for long minutes, her breath misting the glass. Nothing.

Convincing herself she'd imagined it, Zoey turned the key in the back door, drew all the curtains, and went to put the kettle on.

Sipping her comforting tea, she watched the children studiously bent over their drawings. Finley was drawing a scene in outer space, his aliens all elongated blue bodies and antennae, and flying aerodynamically impossible ships leaving purple vapour trails.

Connor's drawing was intriguing – a small boat, sailing away into a sunset over the ocean, and a boy tending the sail, with a shaggy, long-haired dog sitting next to him. Dolphins swam beside the boat.

Zoey smiled; it was good, it was better than good. Not for the first time she wondered about her brother's future – if maybe being an artist was in the cards for him.

As for Megan's drawing, Zoey paused, looking more closely, her brows drawing together in concern. In Megan's childish rendition, Zoey could make out a car and two stick people lying on the ground, with a third, smaller figure kneeling beside them.

A tall, menacing stick figure was standing before them, arm outstretched, something held in its hand, a dark hat pulled over its head.

Tall, looming trees had been drawn in the background, and there, hiding behind one of them, was another figure.

Watching.

Waiting.

Zoey shivered, something about that stick figure sending chills down her spine.

"Who's that, Megan?" she asked, pointing to the hidden figure.

Megan startled, looking at her drawing as if becoming aware of it for the first time. Then she grabbed the black crayon and scribbled desperately until the figure was covered.

"Megan, sweetheart, it's okay," Zoey cuddled the child close, as Megan's lip trembled down, and she gripped Brewster fiercely to her chest.

"It's okay, don't worry, everything's okay..."

The lights went out.

Megan cried out in sharp distress, burrowing her head into Zoey's chest, and the boys stared at her wide-eyed in shock.

The kitchen was dimly lit now only by the candle in the middle of the table, and Zoey hurried to reassure.

"It's okay, don't worry, it's the storm, it's blown the wires together outside. Don't worry. Look, we'll light some more candles, and everything will be fine."

Prising herself free of Megan, she moved swiftly to the dresser drawer and pulled out more candles. Hurrying about the kitchen, she placed and lit them all, until warming flames leapt, and the children's faces relaxed in the glow.

"I'll be back in a moment," she promised.

Taking a candle, she went into the hall to the front door. Opening it, she peered outside, able to see that the other houses in the street were all lit up as normal.

Re-entering the kitchen, that feeling was back. The sensation that something bad was about to happen, squirming in her stomach.

Swallowing her fear, she smiled brightly at them.

"Tell you what, I'll phone Marcus, see where he and mum have got to."

Fumbling the note out from under the phone, she squinted to see the numbers in the semi-light, and carefully dialled them.

Ages, it took ages for him to pick up.

She was on the point of giving up when he answered, his voice husky and breathless.

"Zoey, it's okay, we've nearly finished, we'll be home soon. How's Megan, is she…?"

"Marcus, can you come home, please. I really think you need to come home now!"

"What? Zoey? What's the matter?"

His voice went into echo and suddenly Mum was there.

"Zoey, love? What's wrong?"

"Mum."

Trying and failing to hide her fear, Zoey could hear it in her voice and felt the children behind her lay down their crayons, creeping from their chairs to huddle behind her.

"The lights have all gone out, but I don't think it's the storm. I can see lights on in the neighbour's house. It's only ours."

"It's an old fuse box, honey," Mum reassured. "It might have tripped.'

"I know." Zoey's reply was taut with apprehension. "But I don't think that's it…"

She paused and heard it, a thud below her feet.

She gasped.

It came from the cellar.

There was a split second of silence when they all strained to hear, terror etched on the children's faces, then the sound of breaking glass.

"Zoey!" Mum cried down the line. "What is it? What's happened?"

"I think there's someone in the house," Zoey whispered, and the line went dead.

Zoey froze, clutching the phone and staring at the floor. She knew exactly what it was that something, or someone, had knocked over in the cellar.

Never one to throw anything away, Grace had stored the panes of glass from the old back door down there, propped up against the wall, planning to make a cold frame from them one day.

Zoey had seen them only last week when she helped Mum store the garden harvest down there. She had even commented on how dangerous it was, the way the panes were angled, and could remember her mum's laughing reply.

"Well, you and I are the only ones who ever come down here, and we know where they are."

Now someone else was in the cellar.

Someone who hadn't known to be careful.

Zoey remembered the fuse board was also down there and that the telephone wire entered the house at that point.

Galvanised into action, she dropped the phone and grabbed Megan's hand.

"We have to go," she insisted. "Now! Come on, quickly."

Dragging Megan across the floor, she heard the boys following, for once not arguing.

At the kitchen door, she hesitated.

They needed to get to where other people were – the street, their neighbours – any of them would take them in, would call the police, would help.

"Quickly," she urged again, fumbling the kitchen door open and pulling them through.

The door to the cellar was under the stairs, next to the kitchen.

She glanced at it.

The door handle was softly, silently, turning.

Her hair stood on end and her heart stopped.

"Zoey," whimpered Finley; he saw it too.

"Back!" she urged through gritted teeth, almost tripping over Megan in her desperate need to push them back into the kitchen.

Slamming the door shut, she locked it. But the lock was flimsy; she knew it wouldn't hold for long.

"Out!" she ordered.

"Where?" gasped Connor.

"Garden."

"But ... it's dark, the storm."

"Go! Now!"

Almost pulling Megan's arm out of its socket, she dragged the little girl who was crying in sheer terror, over to the back door and fumbled with the key.

She glanced back as a kick reverberated on the door. He was trying to kick it in. Was trying to get to them.

The lock shifted, but held, buying them precious seconds as she finally forced the stiff key around in her clammy hands and threw the door open.

"Out!" she ordered again, pushing them all before her.

They jumped as a shot echoed behind them, and the kitchen door exploded into the room in a shower of glass from the panes and splinters of wood.

He had a gun!

He'd shot the lock!

"Run!" Zoey ordered.

The children obeyed.

Terrified, they fled into the night. Knowing the garden like the back of their hands even in the dark, the twins raced like gazelles to the vegetable plot, instinctively trying to put as much distance as possible between them and their pursuer.

Zoey scooped up Megan as she tripped and fell, sprawling on the ground with a scream of shock. Slinging the little girl onto her hip, Zoey ran after the boys, catching up with them by the apple tree.

"Where?" gasped Connor.

"Up the ladder," she ordered. "Take Megan, pull the ladder up behind you."

"What about you?" he begged, as Finley began to climb.

Wrenching a reluctant Megan from her chest, where she was clinging like an octopus, Zoey put her high up on the rungs of the ladder.

"I'll distract him, draw him away. If you keep quiet, he'll never know you're up there."

"No, Zoey, he's got a gun, he'll kill you."

"He'll have to catch me first," assured Zoey. "Now go, quickly."

Without another word, Connor swarmed up the ladder like a monkey pushing Megan before him onto the balcony, then both boys pulled the ladder up and away.

Heart pounding painfully in her ears, Zoey took a great, silent step away from the tree, and listened. The fierce need to protect her brothers and Megan welled up inside until she was bathed in fury.

How dare this man come into their home and threaten them? How dare he bring a gun to hurt them with?

Where was he?

Standing.

Listening.

All Zoey could hear was the wild howling of the wind, the branches thrashing all around the garden, the sound of the nearby fence creaking and groaning in the gale.

~Chapter Twenty-One~
"No one threatens my family,"

Zoey wondered how long it would take for Marcus and Mum to get here. Wondered if they had called the police. Wondered how long they would take to respond.

Too long.

He was here, now.

And she had to deal with him.

Taking another silent step forward back to the house, away from the tree and the children, Zoey cried out as a huge figure suddenly loomed up out of the dark and a large hand grabbed for her.

Twisting, she felt him snatch at her, her hair ripping out in his hand as he grabbed at her ponytail.

Gasping with shock, she dived sideways, and the gun spat in the darkness, its shocking retort almost swallowed by the ever-worsening storm.

Falling to her knees in the mud, Zoey had never felt so scared in all her life, and she desperately tried to clear the panic from her brain.

Think Zoe! Her brain screamed to itself.

Think, think, think!

Staggering back to her feet, she fell against the side of the chicken coop, her senses totally disorientated by fear and the pitch darkness.

Calm down, she screamed to herself, she knew this garden, he didn't.

She had the advantage and knew all the hiding places.

He couldn't see her.

She had to remember that.

He *couldn't* see her.

As if to taunt her the moon – until then hidden behind thickly dense clouds – sailed free of its downy prison, a shaft of moonlight illuminating the garden.

He was there!

Right *there*!

Standing before her, he pointed the gun straight at her. Zoey began to violently shake, her terror consuming any rational thought.

Trapped against the wire fence, she had nowhere to go and stared at the end of his gun. He was going to shoot her, was going to kill her.

Here.

Now.

And then he'd find the children and shoot them too.

"Where's the kid?" he snarled, pitching his voice to be heard over the wind.

"What? What kid?"

Confused, she stuttered out the words, not understanding what he wanted.

"The girl, Megan, where is she?" His harsh, American accent grated.

"I … I don't know … not here…"

"Don't lie, I was following, saw them come here, saw him leave alone. So, where is she?"

"Why … why do you want her?"

"It was gonna be the guy," he said. "Just the guy, but there was the woman as well. She got in the way. I didn't mean to shoot her; she was an accident, cos I don't usually shoot women."

Dragging together her scattered thoughts, Zoey realised he was talking about the carjacking.

In the persistent harsh moonlight, she saw his face, the tiny goatee beard, the hat pulled low over his eyes.

"Then there was a kid crying, but I don't waste kids, that's not what I do, no matter how many times he ordered me to, I don't waste kids. So, he threatened her, told her if she ever talked then I'd find her, kill her too."

"Who? Who threatened her?"

"So, I'm gonna ask you nicely one more time. Where's Megan?"

"What are you going to do to her?" Zoey gasped, her knees shaking so badly they could barely support her.

"She's talking now, could identify me, so a promise is a promise."

"I thought you said you didn't kill kids!"

"Yeah, well," he grinned evilly. "There's always a first time for everything."

He levelled the gun at her, and Zoey realised he meant to kill her too because now she could identify him as well.

She sobbed in fear as she looked down the barrel of his gun and time seemed to stand still.

Suddenly, a growling, snarling, battering ram of black and white fur launched itself out of the darkness.

His jaws closing over the man's arm, Badger knocked him to the ground, rolling over with the yelling, kicking, screaming figure.

Zoey ran as the moon sailed again behind the clouds and the garden was draped in darkness.

Behind her, she heard a single gunshot, a whimper, then silence.

Badger!

Oh, Badger.

Tripping over something in the dark, she fumbled for it and found her beekeeping hat, forgotten, left where she had dropped it earlier.

Scrambling to her feet, an idea flashed through her mind, and she angled towards the furthest corner of the garden.

Deliberately, she ran into the open and allowed him to see her, then darted back. With a great yell of rage, he followed her.

Creeping behind the compost heap, she pulled on the beekeeping hat, dragging its long veil down as far as possible.

Silently, she crouched behind the hives and waited, her heart pounding. She listened to him thrashing about the undergrowth until once again the moon's clothes were ripped from its silvery, blushing face and the garden was illuminated.

She stood up.

He saw her, saw the fence behind her, and realised she had nowhere else to go. He walked towards her, slowly and deliberately.

"Now come on, don't be stupid. Tell me where she is and maybe we can come to some sort of arrangement."

He stopped, noticing the hat for the first time.

"What's that? Hey, what's that on your head?"

Swiftly, Zoey kicked at one of the hives, shifting it forward on its stand. She kicked again. This time it toppled, rolling over towards him.

Desperately, she kicked at the other one, sending it flying.

Shoving her hands deep into her pockets she stood still, calming her aura, trying to project the soothing thoughts she always had when tending the bees, her bees.

The same bees who had tried to warn her this was coming.

"Hey!" he cried again. "What are you doing …? What the … no … get off … get off!"

Maddened by the destruction of their hives, the bees swarmed angrily in the storm, and Zoey felt them fly all around her.

Staying calm and still, she sent positive thoughts their way and felt a few buzzing around her netted face, before flying away to where he was flailing and flapping his hands, swatting them away, making himself a target, making them angrier.

Zoey listened in sick fascination as his cries of anger turned to screams of pain and fear.

The bees swarmed, their hive minds transmitting the threat of him to their fellows until he was one, great, heaving mass of small bodies.

Saddened by the bees' sacrifice, Zoey knew how many would die.

Slowly, carefully, she took a step to the right, and then another, until she was at the shed. Fumbling at its door, she reached in and grabbed the solid garden spade from its place against the wall.

Her steps slow and precise she crossed to where he had fallen to the ground, his mouth an open shriek of agony.

"Help me!" he screamed when he glimpsed her through eyes almost swollen shut from multiple stings.

"Please, help me!"

Zoey lifted the spade.

"No one threatens my family," she said and brought the spade down.

~Chapter Twenty-Two~
"He died saving your sister,"

"I think there's someone in the house," Zoey whispered, and then the line went dead.

"Zoey!" cried Grace. Marcus checked the signal, the battery, both fine, Zoey had just gone. "Get her back," Grace yelled, clutching his arm.

"I can't, she disconnected her end, or…"

"Or?!"

"Someone disconnected for her."

For a heartbeat they stared at one another, then Grace beat him to the door, ripping it almost off its hinges in her haste to get out.

"Grace!" he called when she set off in the wrong direction. "Car!"

Confused, she spun around and caught up with him as he raced towards the Jag, pulling his keys from his pocket, and tossing her the phone as she scrambled into the passenger seat beside him.

"Call the police," he ordered. "Tell them there's a possible break-in, give them the address, tell them there are children there, alone."

"Zoey," she sobbed.

"Is still a child," he snapped, grimly.

Quickly, she did as he ordered, dialling 999, asking for the police and briefly and precisely giving them all the details.

"They're on their way," she gasped, her hand flying to her chest as if to calm her pounding heart.

"Good," he said, concentrating on the road and the traffic which was thankfully sparse due to the storm. Cursing, he yanked on the wheel, pulling the car abruptly to the kerb.

"What ...?" yelped Grace, bracing herself against the dashboard.

"Look."

He gestured ahead, opening his door. A telegraph pole lay across the road in front of the car mere inches from the bonnet.

"We have to get past," she cried, following him from the car, the wind whipping the words from her mouth and tossing them up into the air.

"Nothing's getting past that," he retorted. Easing cautiously past the dangling wires, he held out his hand and helped her to scramble up the bank and over a low hedge into someone's front garden, across the leaf scattered lawn and over the hedge on the other side.

"Which way?" he asked, helping her down, back onto the road.

"This way." She pointed into the darkness; their path barely lit by flickering streetlights.

Following her at a jog, Marcus remembered the fear in Zoey's voice and prayed they weren't too late.

When they reached the house some ten minutes later it was dark and silent.

Too dark.

Too silent.

Pulling her key out, Grace let them in with a shaking hand. Before he could stop her, she called out loudly.

"Zoey?"

"Hush," he snapped.

"Why?"

"If there is someone in the house, we don't want to let them know we're here."

Subsiding into silence, her eyes wide, Grace let him push her to one side and sidle cautiously in ahead of her.

Looking around the almost pitch-dark hall, he saw light glimmering at the end, candlelight, flickering in the kitchen.

Softly, he eased his way forward and saw the cellar door standing open. Glancing at it, he noted the bolts at the top and bottom.

Quietly, he closed the door and slid the bolts, not sure if he was doing any good, but instantly feeling better once that gaping black hole was secured.

Beside him, Grace sucked in her breath and pulled at his sleeve, pointing at the kitchen door. He looked and saw what she was drawing his attention to.

The door was shattered, splinters of wood scattered on the floor, glass from the panes littered far into the room.

It looked almost as if...

Swallowing hard, Marcus kept his thoughts to himself and pushed on the broken door, edging into the candlelit kitchen, Grace close on his heels.

The candles were mostly out, only a few of the more sheltered ones still flickered. The rest had been blown out by the wind that gusted through the wide-open back door. Outside, the darkness beckoned.

"Do you have a torch?" he whispered.

Grace nodded and stepped gingerly past him, her wellies crunching on broken glass and the long wooden splinters that lay everywhere.

Opening the cupboard under the sink, she pulled out a large, sturdy, rubber torch. She handed it to him, and Marcus switched it on with relief.

Its powerful beam cut a swathe through the night as he stepped through the back door, looking cautiously around at the storm-tossed garden, eerily empty.

"Where are they?" Grace cried.

Marcus shook his head, the garden's emptiness sending jitters of unease down his spine.

"Zoey!"

Unable to contain herself any longer, Grace's bellow echoed down the garden.

"Mum, over here..."

Relief gripped them both.

Shining the torch ahead of them they quickly rounded the corner and saw a huddle of figures by the chicken coop.

Indistinguishable in the gloom, they were crouched over something lying on the ground.

Megan?

His heart missed a beat and he almost tripped in the cumbersome wellies in his haste to reach them.

Stumbling, he gratefully accepted Grace's arm as she yanked him back upright.

"Zoey?" she enquired, and Zoey turned from where she was kneeling on the ground, Megan tucked under one arm.

"Mum?"

They could hear from her voice she was crying. Beside her, Megan was sobbing, her shoulders heaving as she patted the form lying still and unmoving on the ground.

"Badger?" Grace cried. "Oh no, Badger!"

"I'm sorry, Mum."

Zoey was crying properly now. Scrambling to her feet she threw herself into her mother's arms.

"He died protecting me. That man was going to shoot me, but Badger attacked him. He gave me time to get away. He saved my life, Mum. Badger saved my life."

Grace enfolded her daughter into her arms, soothing and shushing as her eyes met Marcus's over her daughter's heaving shoulders.

"Zoey," he asked, urgently. "This man, the one who attacked you. Where is he now?"

"Over there."

Zoey gestured vaguely towards the back of the garden.

"The boys are guarding him. Here," she fished in her sweatshirt pocket and to his horror drew out a gun. "You'd better take this."

Taking it gingerly, Marcus flicked the safety on and slipped it into his pocket.

Crouching down by Megan, he gently patted Badger's still warm body, then hugged her to him.

"I'm so sorry about Badger," he said.

Megan nodded, gravely.

"Brave Badger," she said, her little hand stroking and stroking.

"Brave Badger," she said again.

"Yes," he agreed. "Brave Badger. Now, you stay here with Grace while I go and find the boys."

"They're with the bad man," she said as he rose to his feet and peered into the darkness. Grace and Zoey huddled down next to her.

"Poor Badger," said Grace, then looked up at him. "The boys…"

"I'll find them, don't worry," he assured her. "You stay here with the girls and Badger."

She nodded, and he left them there.

"Finley? Connor?"

"Over here," came the reply and he picked his way carefully over to them, watching his feet in the gloom, glad the wind seemed to have reached its peak and was now abating.

The two figures stood in the darkness, waiting for him. Shining his torch onto their faces, he saw their twin expressions of mingled concern, relief, and pride.

"We got him," Connor, or it might have been Finley, announced, once he was near enough to hear. "He came to get Megan, but we got him instead."

"Zoey got him," his twin insisted, and his brother shrugged away the semantics.

"Anyway, we helped tie him up, and we've been guarding him so Zoey and Megan could stay with Badger."

His lip quivered down.

"Is Badger … is he?"

"I'm so sorry, guys," Marcus said gently. "I'm afraid the poor old boy is dead."

The twins exchanged glances.

"We thought he must be," Connor said. "When Zoey told us he'd been shot, we knew, Fin and me, we knew he'd probably be dead."

Their faces trembled in shared grief and Marcus stepped closer, engulfing their sturdy bodies, one under each arm.

"He died saving your sister," he reassured, feeling them sob against his arms. "Saving you all."

In the distance, they heard the wail of sirens, and the boys straightened up. Their grief at the death of their old dog pushed to one side in their excitement at the evening's events.

"Is that the police?" asked Connor. "Only, I think the bad man might need an ambulance as well."

Confused, Marcus shone the torch down onto the man's face and saw him clearly for the first time, recoiling at the reddened swollen flesh, the slits of eyes, and the gaping, bleeding gash across the side of the man's head.

"Good lord!" he exclaimed. "What on earth did your sister do to him?"

"She set her bees on him," answered Connor, proudly. "He tried to shoot her, so she told her bees to attack him, and they did."

"Told the bees…?"

"Well, it wasn't exactly like that," admitted Finley. "She sort of kicked the hives over, and that made the bees angry, so they attacked him."

"Bees did all this?"

"Well, Zoey hit him with the spade as well. I think she only knocked him out though. I don't think she killed him." Sounding almost disappointed about this, Finley continued.

"Then she tied him up, took his gun and came and got us from the treehouse where we'd been hiding. Then we stood guard over him, ready to give him a whack if he woke up."

For the first time, Marcus noticed the spade gripped tightly in Connor's hand.

"And then Zoey and Megan went to see about Badger, and then you came."

Thinking that Zoey sounded like a bloody hero, one fully deserving of a medal, Marcus eased the boys away from the prone body on the ground.

"Come on, guys, let's go and let the police in and let them take him away."

"He might escape," Finley protested.

Marcus looked down at the broken, battered, and bound body.

"You know what, boys, I don't think he's going anywhere. Come on, let's go and talk to the police."

~Chapter Twenty-Three~
"Shall we see you again soon?"

"Tell me about Badger." It was later that evening, much later. The police had finally gone after talking to Zoey for what seemed hours and taking statements from them all.

Marcus and Grace listened with ever-mounting horror as she told them how the man had cornered her, pointed a gun at her, and admitted he was there to kill Megan because she could identify him as her parents' murderer.

Giving the police inspector the telephone number of his counterpart in New York, Marcus was assured they would liaise with them about this. That they would let the American police know their case was now closed. That Monica and Walter's murderer was now in custody and was currently being treated for a fractured skull, concussion, and a reaction to bee stings.

The inspector had blinked at this, looking at Zoey with respect as she told him how she lured the killer down to her beehives, then angered the bees by kicking them over.

"How did you know they wouldn't sting you as badly as they stung him?" The inspector asked, and Zoey shrugged.

"I didn't, not really. I had the hat on so I knew that would protect me from the worst of it, and I knew to stand still, not flap around. Also, the bees know me, I look after them, I didn't think they'd harm me."

"But you didn't know for sure?"

"No," she agreed. "I didn't know for sure."

After the police left, Zoey and Grace swept the kitchen floor whilst Marcus and the boys retrieved poor Badger's body.

Wrapping it in an old towel, they placed it in the shed ready for burial in the morning.

Deciding they were all starving, Marcus ordered fish and chips to be delivered. The boys' eyes growing wide with greed at such an unexpected treat.

Even Megan managed to eat some before her eyes drooped with tiredness. Zoey snuggled her down on the old sofa, tucking blankets around her, and placing a pillow under her head.

"She doesn't want to be alone," she informed the others, and they were all silent in their agreement.

None of them wanted to be alone that night.

Now they were still sitting at the table, glasses of wheat and dandelion wine in front of the adults, which Marcus decided was not that bad.

It had been assumed with no words being necessary, that Marcus and Megan would be staying that night, and he had texted Luke to let him know.

"So," he said again. "Tell me about Badger."

"Badger?"

Grace smiled a sad smile of memory.

"He was a rescue dog," said Finley.

"Mum rescued him, from a circus..."

"No, you're telling it all wrong," insisted Zoey, and looked at her mother.

"You tell it, Mum, you tell it the best."

"Badger," sighed Grace. "I found him fifteen years ago when I was heavily pregnant with Zoey. I was living in a hostel with a load of other single mothers-to-be, strictly no pets allowed."

She paused and took a sip of wine, then looked at them all seated around the table, listening to her tell the tale.

"The circus had been to town. I hadn't been, of course, no money, and anyway I hate circuses, but the next day I went for a walk down to the green where they'd been. I was roaming about, looking at all the litter that had been dropped, when I heard this whimpering noise."

"It was like this," said Finley, snuffling a bit with his cold as he made whimpering noises.

"He didn't sound like that," his twin scoffed.

"Did too."

"Didn't."

"Boys," cautioned their mother mildly. "Do you want me to tell you the story, or not?"

"Sorry, Mum," they murmured in unison.

"So, I heard this whimpering, and I looked all around, but couldn't find anything. Then, I noticed this big bag of rubbish over by the dustbins. The noise seemed to be coming from there, so I went over to investigate. And that's where I found him. Tied up in a bin bag and left for the dustmen to take away, was this tiny husky puppy with beautiful blue eyes and black and white markings on his face."

"He looked like a badger," broke in Connor.

"So that's why Mum called him Badger," confirmed Finley.

"I see," said Marcus. "Do you think the circus people had put him in the bag deliberately?"

"Who knows?" Grace shrugged and yawned. "Maybe they did, maybe it was an accident, maybe he crawled in there by himself after some food that had been thrown away, we'll never know. But anyway, I brought him back to the hostel and smuggled him in."

"How did you manage to hide him?" Marcus asked.

Grace smiled at the memory.

"The other girls. They completely fell in love with this tiny scrap, and all chipped in to help. They saved their money to buy him food, and we all took turns cleaning up after him and hiding him whenever the staff were around."

"And he's been with you ever since?"

"Yes, he loved us all," said Zoey. "But he was always Mum's dog. I don't think he ever forgot that she saved his life.

"And tonight, he saved the lives of your children." Marcus looked at Grace, her eyes were swimming with tears, but she smiled and nodded. "He repaid his debt to you and died a hero's death protecting the family he loved, and who have loved and looked after him all his life."

He lifted his glass of wine.

"To Badger."

The others lifted their glasses.

"To Badger," they chorused.

The next morning, Marcus and Megan stood on the doorstep to say goodbye, Marcus having slipped out earlier to retrieve his abandoned car.

No one had wanted to sleep alone, so Zoey and Megan had slept with Grace, and Marcus had slept on a mattress on the floor with the twins.

Lying awake most of the night listening to their even breathing, he wondered about Grace.

More specifically, about him and Grace.

If Zoey hadn't called. If they hadn't been interrupted, how far would they have gone, and what would it have meant?

More to her than it did to him?

Probably.

He knew Grace wasn't the kind of woman to sleep around, had probably not been involved with any other man since Daniel.

She was lonely, the situation had been unusual, that was all.

In hindsight, it was probably just as well nothing had happened.

It made things less ... complicated.

Less ... messy.

It made it easier to walk away, to leave her and her children behind.

Because there was no other option. Not wanting to hurt her with a brief fling, Marcus decided to nip it in the bud. It was kinder that way, easier...

After all, he couldn't have long-term feelings for Grace. They lived in very different worlds, and it was time he returned to his.

Spending more time with her, with the children, would only give her hope that he ... that they ... and he didn't, because it wasn't possible.

But he liked her too much to want to hurt her, so it was better if he went now, and never came back.

He glanced up at the house, thinking how the next time he saw it would be the day he and Megan moved in.

~175~

He wondered what it would be like to live here. What the house would feel like without the Lovejoys in it.

She smiled at him, but he refused to see the hope behind it, the question her eyes were asking.

"Thank you," she said. "For everything."

Thank you for bringing a madman into our lives who nearly murdered my kids, his mind couldn't help adding.

"Shall we see you again soon?"

There it was.

The hope was blatant, her assumption that he ... that they...

Marcus knew he had to make the cut surgical sharp and definite.

"Probably not," he replied, crisply and dismissively.

"I think it's best we let the estate agents handle things from now on. I'll make the arrangements with my solicitors, and they'll get the ball rolling."

Her face dropped, the smile faded, and he saw the light dim in her eyes.

She nodded, understanding what he was saying, what he was doing.

"Okay," she agreed. "Whatever you think is best."

Unaware of his rejection of their mother, the boys swarmed over him, hugging his legs, and even hugging Megan, much to her delight.

"Bye, Megan, bye Marcus," they chimed. "See you soon."

He didn't have the heart to correct them.

Zoey knew though.

Silently, she looked him up and down, her face stiff with disapproval. Bending down, she hugged Megan fiercely.

"You take care," she whispered.

"I'll see you soon, Zoey," Megan replied, happily confident that the Lovejoys would always be a part of her life.

Straightening up, Zoey shot him a look of intense dislike and maybe disappointment, then turned on her heel and went back into the house.

With Megan waving goodbye from the back seat, Marcus edged the car out into morning traffic, and they drove away.

Back to the city and the life he had left behind there.

At Luke's, cups of fresh coffee in front of them, he told them of the night's events whilst Lucia and Megan ran about the garden collecting fallen leaves and other debris from the storm.

They listened intently, Arianna gasping in horror as he told of the gunman tracking down the children in the storm, of the amazing heroism of Zoey, and the man's confession to the murder of Monica and Walter.

"Do you think he was the one who set fire to your flat?" Luke asked shrewdly.

Marcus shrugged.

"I don't know, maybe, I know the police are questioning him about that. It would make sense he would try to make it look like an accidental death first."

"And he would have succeeded," murmured Arianna. "If not for a little girl with chickenpox, and a little girl who wanted to be a bridesmaid."

"Yes," Marcus agreed, and they all fell silent, faces sombre at the thought of the whims of life.

Marcus phoned his mother to tell her it was over. That the man who had murdered her daughter had been caught, and that he would pay for his actions.

Listening to his mother sob with relief, he realised how lonely she must be sometimes.

Her only family in America had been Monica and Walter and, of course, Megan, and now they had all been taken away from her.

"Would you like us to come over for a visit, Mum?"

"What?"

"Megan and me? Shall we come for a visit, to see you. After all, you haven't seen Megan for several months and she's always talking about you. I know she'd love to see you."

"Really? You'll come?"

"Yes, now's a perfect time, before we move into our new home."

"What about work? I know how busy you are."

"I can delegate, and I can check in with the New York office whilst I'm there. It doesn't hurt to keep them on their toes."

"Then yes, I would simply love to see you both, if you think you can spare the time."

"You're my family, Mum, I'll always spare the time for family."

~Chapter Twenty-Four~
"He left and he's not coming back"

In the days leading up to their departure for New York, Marcus found himself slipping back into his old, pre-Megan ways, because it was easier that way. It meant he didn't have to think or feel about anything.

He spent long days at the office, leaving before Megan was awake and often getting home long after she had gone to bed. He told himself he was clearing the backlog before they left for New York and reassured himself that she was fine in the excellent care of Luke and Arianna.

Not wanting to talk to anyone, he was silent and morose at the dinner table, slipping away into a world of his own whilst the conversation ebbed and flowed around him.

Then it was time to go. Luke drove them to the airport, his brother seemingly out of words for once. Marcus felt his penetrating, thoughtful gaze rest on him often during the drive, but Luke decided to keep his thoughts to himself.

Settling into the guestroom of his mother's three-storey brownstone in one of the nicer New York districts and listening to the excited chatter of Megan reunited with her grandmother, he thought about never going back.

He could do up the house and sell it straight on – probably make a tidy profit. He could buy something more suitable for him and Megan here. It made sense.

His mother was here. Megan's old school would gladly take her back, so she'd be with her friends again. As for work, he could easily promote a manager to do his job in London and run the company from the New York branch.

It was all ... doable. Marcus thought about leaving Britain, of moving here and taking up the American side of his heritage, of leaving Luke and the rest of his family behind. Yes, moving here might be the best thing for Megan. But was it the best thing for him?

Unable to think through the fog of lethargy that seemed to surround him these days, Marcus left the idea alone, consigning it to the ever-growing pile of things that needed to be thought about at some time, but not now.

The days drifted. Busying himself at work, he found it helped if you didn't think too much about anything. Especially about things left behind. Things that had once been within his grasp. Things that had felt important to him, but ultimately were things that had been discarded, considered not worth the keeping.

Thousands of miles away across an ocean, Zoey seriously considered slapping her mother or shaking her, or yelling at her.

Anything to snap her out of this distracted, unmotivated mood she had been wandering around in ever since...

Well, ever since *he* had left.

Official looking solicitor's letters had arrived making it all seem terrifyingly real, and Zoey had bullied and forced her mother into completing the forms. Signing on the dotted line and agreeing to sell their home to Marcus for a sum of money that had made Zoey blink and wonder how rich he was.

Nothing had been done about finding them a new home. Not a single thing had been sorted or packed, and Zoey was reaching the limits of her patience.

"Mum, where are we going to go?"

She finally snapped one afternoon on coming home from school to find her mother still sitting at the table, a cold cup of tea before her, and no sign she had done anything at all since Zoey left that morning.

"Things are in motion, the house is going to be sold but we've got nowhere to go yet, the place is a tip, and you're sitting there, drinking tea!"

Enough was enough. It was time, Zoey decided, for cold, hard truth to be dispensed.

Her mother blinked, looked around, then smiled that vague, not-quite-in-the-room smile she had been smiling so much lately.

"Hi sweetie, you're home early."

"I'm not early, it's gone four o'clock." Zoey gritted her teeth in despair. "Where are the boys? They should be home by now."

"Oh, Oliver's mum called, they've gone there to play. I'll need to go and pick them up soon.'

She noticed the folded cardboard boxes in Zoey's hand. "What are they for?"

"We need to start sorting this place out and get packing, mum. Wherever we end up is going to be heaps smaller than this, so we need to start getting rid of stuff. I thought we could start this evening, so I got these boxes from Mr Patel's on the high street, along with some bin bags for all the rubbish we'll be chucking out."

"Oh, there's plenty of time, love. No need to worry about it tonight."

"Yes, we do need to start worrying about it. Mum, what's the matter with you? We'll move out and have nowhere to go unless you get off your backside and start looking."

Zoey wanted to cry. Tired of being the adult, she wanted her mum back; that tireless, powerhouse of a woman who worked endlessly and always knew what to do.

Zoey hated the woman her mum had become, drifting through her days aimlessly, merely existing in the moment, not thinking ahead, not planning for anything. Angrily flicking on the kettle, Zoey stomped to the fridge only to discover there was no milk. Staring in disbelief at the empty carton that had been put back in the door, she rounded on her mother.

"Right, that's it! I've had enough. Put your shoes on, go and get the boys, and get some milk on your way back. And tonight, we're going to start sorting this house out, cos you might be okay with the idea of us sleeping in a cardboard box on the street, but I'm not."

Startled by her daughter's outburst, Grace slowly rose to her feet.

"I'm sorry," she murmured. "I don't know what's the matter with me lately, I don't seem able to focus on anything."

"It's all right, mum." Feeling guilty, Zoey hugged her mother. "I understand, I really do.

But he left and he's not coming back, so you might as well accept it and move on."

Grace stared at her. "You think I'm like this because I'm missing Marcus?"

"Well, aren't you?"

"No," Grace snorted, sounding more like her old, feisty self. "Nothing of the sort. There was never anything between us to miss. Yes, he was nice enough, and he was kind to us all, but I wasn't in love with him or anything."

Zoey merely watched as her mother located her shoes from under the table, pulled them on and took her bag down from the peg.

"But you're right, Zoey," she said from the door. "It is time to move on. Maybe the boys and I will stop at the estate agents on the way back, get some details, see what's out there."

"Good idea," said Zoey, sighing as her mother left and wondering if she'd even remember to collect the boys, let alone the milk.

Left alone, Zoey looked around the cluttered, untidy kitchen, and decided to make a start herself. Shaking out a bin bag, she went through the cupboards like a thing possessed, throwing away anything she didn't think they could take to their new home. Wherever that might be.

Shaking out her fourth bin bag, she started on the kitchen table, shaking her head at the amount of crud that had accumulated on both it and the crammed full dresser against the wall.

Locating a pile of the boys' drawings, she decided to be ruthless and chuck the lot, then had second thoughts, figuring she better have a quick look through them first, not wanting to throw away any masterpieces.

Smiling, she flicked through them, pulling out some to keep, tossing most in the bin bag until she reached one that she recognised immediately. Surveying the stick figures lying on the ground, the figure with the gun, the trees in the background, and the black crayon scribble where that second figure had lurked, she realised she had never told anyone about him – not Marcus, not Mum, not the police.

She had never told them the attacker had claimed that another man had put him up to it.

Thinking furiously, cursing herself for her stupidity, Zoey wondered what to do.

Do nothing? After all, everything was okay now, the attacker was in prison, Megan was safe ... Unease crept down Zoey's spine. A feeling that everything was not all right, was very far from being all right. That things were very, very wrong.

Sitting there, staring at Megan's drawing, a growing conviction crept over Zoey that she had to tell Marcus about this now, this minute. That something terrible would happen if she didn't.

Locating the scrap of paper with his number, she anxiously dialled it. She knew he was in New York – the estate agent had mentioned it the last time she had called – and briefly, Zoey wondered about time differences, then decided it didn't matter.

She would wake him up if she had to, this was too important to wait.

~Chapter Twenty-Five~
"Marcus! She's gone!"

Sipping his mid-morning coffee, Marcus thought how much he missed Sally. His PA in New York was perfectly adequate, but she wasn't Sally.

Used to the working relationship they had developed over many years, and the fact Sally at times seemed to have mind-reading capabilities – anticipating his needs before he even knew what they were himself – he missed her dreadfully.

He wondered if he did decide to relocate to New York, whether he could persuade Sally to come too.

His mobile rang as he was about to take another sip and he muttered in annoyance, carefully replaced the cup in the saucer, and glanced at the caller ID.

It was Grace's number.

For a moment he considered ignoring it, simply letting it go to voicemail and finding out what she wanted first.

It was tempting.

Then he felt mean and small for even considering fobbing her off like that.

Not after all she had done for him, for Megan.

"Grace?"

"No, it's Zoey."

"Zoey? What is it? Is everything okay? Is your mum all right?"

"Other than being a right procrastinating pain in the arse, yes, she's fine. That's not why I'm calling."

The smile that had begun to spread at her description of Grace faltered at the tight concern he heard in her voice.

"What is it? What's the matter?"

"Marcus, I'm sorry, I should have told you, but I kind of forgot, what with everything that happened, and Badger, and well, everything."

"Told me what?"

"That night, the night it happened, before he broke in, the kids were busy drawing and Megan drew a picture of her parents' murder."

"What?"

"Right down to the last detail, the car, her mum and dad lying on the ground, her kneeling beside them, the attacker pointing a gun at her, she even drew his hat."

"Maybe it was her way of coping with it," suggested Marcus, slowly.

"Maybe," Zoey agreed, impatiently. "But that's not all. Megan drew somebody else at the scene, someone hiding in the trees, watching the attack. And later, when that man pointed a gun at me, he said there was only supposed to have been a man, that a woman was there and she wasn't supposed to be, so he had to shoot her because she got in the way."

"Monica," murmured Marcus.

"Exactly, and he said there was a kid, Megan, but he didn't want to waste the kid, that that's not what he did, so the other man threatened Megan, told her if she ever spoke of it, ever told anyone about them, that they'd find her and shoot her."

Marcus shook his head in stunned disbelief, unable to get his head around what she was telling him.

"Zoey, are you sure about this?"

"Absolutely," she replied, her conviction ringing like truth down the line.

"And my thinking is, whoever planned the attack on Megan's parents wasn't expecting anyone to be with her dad. They didn't know Megan and her mum were going to be with him. So, it was someone who wanted her dad dead, and only him."

Marcus's thoughts were flying now, trying, and failing, to spot a flaw in her logic.

"Then, Megan gets spooked into talking again so they had to shut her up. But how did they know she was talking? Who told them? Not many people knew, and your flat was torched only days after she started speaking."

"The police don't know if that was arson or not yet ..." Marcus broke in.

"Of course, it was arson!"

Zoey huffed incredulously.

"He was trying to shut Megan up before she said anything to incriminate him. Then he tried the more direct route and sent his goon to finish her off, once and for all."

"Who did?"

"The other man," Zoey explained patiently. "The man behind the tree. A man who needed to get Megan's dad out of the way. A man who stands to lose everything if he's caught. A man who's probably desperate right now because his plan didn't work, because Megan's still alive and could identify him at any moment..."

When Zoey had gone, after much reassurance from him that he would take care of things, that he would talk to the police on this end and tell them her theory, Marcus sat and thought it all through.

His gut feeling was that Zoey was right. The original attack had been intended for Walter, and Walter alone.

He remembered his mother telling him the decision to make it a family weekend, for Monica and Megan to accompany him, had been last minute.

As far as anyone else was concerned, Walter should have been alone on that quiet country road.

His intercom buzzed, and Adele, his adequate PA, broke into his thoughts, her flat, nasal New York accent sounding concerned.

"Marcus, I have your mother on line one, she seems very distressed about something."

Oh, heavens, what now, he thought, reaching for the handset.

"Mum?"

"Marcus! She's gone!"

"What? Who's gone?"

"Megan! She's gone, she's been kidnapped!"

Time stopped. Marcus gripped the handset, his brain failing to make sense of it all. Zoey's words flashed through his mind – "A man who's probably desperate right now because his plan didn't work, because Megan's still alive, could identify him at any moment..."

Desperate enough to kidnap her? Desperate enough to kill her?

"Calm down, Mum, tell me what happened?"

"We went out first thing, did a little shopping. She needed new shoes because her feet had grown again. When we got back, she asked if she could play in the yard whilst I got us some lunch. I was in the kitchen, I heard her scream, but by the time I got out there, it was too late. The gate was open, and she was gone."

"She may have opened the gate, wandered off by herself?"

"No," interrupted his mother angrily. "I told you, I heard her scream. She was terrified, and she wouldn't leave the yard, not Megan. Besides, she left Brewster lying on the grass."

Marcus's heart sank even further as he acknowledged the truth of his mother's words. Megan wouldn't have wandered off by herself, and she certainly wouldn't have left Brewster behind.

Something else Zoey had said forced its way into his thoughts.

"Mum," he snapped, breaking into her pre-hysterical gasping – needing to stop her before she completely lost it.

"Shut up and listen, this is important. Who did you tell about Megan, that she was talking again?"

"What? No one. Marcus, we need to call the police."

"I know, and we will, but this is important. It could help me to find who's taken her. So, think, Mum, please. Did you tell anyone she was talking again?"

"I don't understand; what does this have to do…"

"Mum!"

Raising his voice for the first time to his mother, he verbally slapped her quiet and waited until her shocked gasps had subsided into quiet whimpers.

"Please," he softened his tone. "Mum, this is so very important. Think! Did you mention it to anyone, anyone at all?"

"Well, no, as I said, no one, there wasn't time, and I didn't see anyone to tell … oh, no one except that odious little man, that is."

"What odious little man?"

Marcus's heart began to pound, a part of him already knowing what name she was going to say.

"That Maxwell Miles character. He called to enquire after Megan, said he'd like to know so he could let Walter's staff know. They were all concerned about her, he said. So, I told him she had started talking again and that we were hopeful she could soon identify the man who did it. Was that wrong, Marcus, why shouldn't I have told him…?"

"Mum don't panic. I think I know who took Megan and I'm going to go and get her back."

"But, Marcus, I don't…"

"I have to go, Mum, I'll call you as soon as I have news."

Hanging up he jumped to his feet, anger pumping through his veins.

That bastard Maxwell!

It had been him all along.

He had arranged for his brother-in-law to be shot down in the street like a dog.

He had had his sister killed for being with her husband.

He who had terrorised a little girl into muteness, and then had sent someone to kill her too.

Storming out of his office, he startled Adele into dropping her coffee, the stain spreading over the cream carpet like a bad mistake.

"Marcus! What...?"

"I need Maxwell Miles's home address, and I need it now!"

"Maxwell who?"

The thought flashed in his mind that Sally would have known and wouldn't have had to ask.

"Maxwell Miles, he's CEO of my brother-in-law's company. His private address, I want it, now!"

Galvanised into action by the urgency in his voice, she snapped to attention, frantically tapping on her keyboard.

Pulling his phone from his pocket, Marcus dialled the number of his contact within the police.

Thankful to reach him immediately, he briefly and concisely told him what had happened.

"This is his address," he added, taking the sheet of paper a now serious-faced Adele quickly handed to him from the printer, reading it out loud.

"I'll meet you there."

"Blackwood, don't do anything stupid, wait for us to get there. Blackwood..."

Marcus hung up, striding towards the door.

"Marcus."

Adele ran on spindly heels to catch up.

"Is there anything else I can do?"

"Phone whoever's on car park duty today, tell them to get my car out of its space and ready to go."

She nodded as he reached the elevators, and the last thing he saw as the doors closed was her putting her phone to her ear.

~Chapter Twenty-Six~
"I guess love makes fools of us all."

Glancing again at the paper Adele had given him, Marcus saw it was an address in Long Island, about an hour away.

Marcus made it in thirty minutes, gunning through traffic, forcing other cars out of his way.

He didn't care.

His powerful car pushed almost to maximum; all he could think about was Megan.

Why had Miles taken her and not simply shot her in the garden?

Too messy?

Maybe?

Perhaps he thought if he took her, he could dispose of her body somewhere and no one would ever know.

Would he be stupid enough to take her to his home?

Maybe.

He was arrogant, thought he was invincible. He didn't know Marcus was onto him.

He thought he was safe, that no one knew of his involvement in Walter and Monica's deaths.

Marcus wondered why he needed Walter out of the way and remembered Walter's strange phone call, elements of it beginning to make sense. He had spoken about having suspicions, about his trust being betrayed.

What had Miles done? Stolen from the company? Marcus knew they dealt with a lot of money. Had Miles been tempted to help himself and somehow Walter had found out.

Yes, that must be it.

He had suspected Miles, but Walter being Walter he had been too cautious, too uncertain, to go directly to the police with his suspicions.

Instead, he phoned Marcus, looking for help in his roundabout, confusing way, but then had abruptly stopped.

Marcus had thought at the time that someone had come in, had that someone been Miles?

Had he overheard, realising that Walter suspected him?

Shaking his head, Marcus decided it could all wait until this was over – until Megan was safe, and Miles in custody.

Let the police do what they liked with him then, all Marcus cared about was Megan.

At the thought of her, terrified, being held prisoner by this man, a cold rage creep up his spine.

Parking on the next block over to Miles' address, he silently walked along a riverside path that ran along the back of the large, generously proportioned houses with their neatly laid out gardens.

Finding the right one, he looked for a way in and saw a gate, obviously intended for access to the pathway he was on. Trying it, he discovered it was locked, bolted on the other side.

Reaching up and over, Marcus blessed his height as his probing fingers found the bolt and gently eased it back.

Pushing it open far enough for him to sidle in, he closed it behind him and darted behind a clump of shrubs off to one side.

Silently moving from one patch of cover to the next, he finally reached the house, rushed to it, and flattened himself against the wall next to the full-length windows opening onto the garden.

Risking a quick peek in, to his relief he saw Megan, sitting on the floor, knees drawn to her chin, rocking in obvious terror.

Of Miles, there was no sign.

Gently, he tried the window.

Locked.

Moving silently along the wall, he spotted the back door, oozed up to it, and tried the handle.

Unlocked.

Concerned it might squeak, he cautiously opened it, inch by painful inch. Sliding into the luxuriously appointed, gleaming kitchen, Marcus took a second to think about the geography of the house as he crept out of the kitchen into a vast hallway and turned left.

Opening the first door he came to he found the lounge and Megan. Relief made him careless.

"Megan," he hissed.

She looked up, her face a mixture of relief and terror. "Uncle Marcus?"

He moved further into the room and bent to pick her up.

"Come on, honey, we're getting out of here."

"But, the bad man, he's here…"

"I know, so we need to go before he gets back."

"No, he's right here."

"Behind you, Blackwood."

Marcus swung around and saw Miles sitting in a chair behind the door, where he had been the whole time, the angle of the room meaning Marcus hadn't seen him from the window.

Cursing his stupidity, Marcus held his hands away from his body as Miles lifted the revolver lying in his lap.

"I should have known you'd guess. It was you he was talking to, wasn't it? On the phone that day? I didn't think he told you anything. I suppose I was wrong."

"No, he didn't have time to tell me anything. I guessed. You were the only person my mother talked to about Megan – that she was talking again. Once I knew that it all fell into place."

Miles nodded, his hands shaking as if the gun was too heavy for him. The burden of what he had done, of what he was about to do, too great.

"Stupid of you to come alone, Blackwood. Strange, I never had you down as a stupid man. But then," he glanced at Megan. "I guess love makes fools of us all."

Outside, Marcus heard the whine of sirens, the sound of car doors, and knew the cavalry had arrived.

"I didn't come alone," he replied. "It's over, Miles. You might as well give yourself up."

"Perhaps," agreed Miles. "But I could still kill you both."

"You could." His voice steady, Marcus fixed his gaze unwaveringly on Miles' face.

"But you know what they do to child killers in jail. Know what they do to men like you? You won't last two minutes, and we both know it. Let us go, maybe a deal can be made."

"A deal?" scoffed Miles. "I arranged to have Walter killed because he found out what I'd done, or at least suspected me of doing. I was desperate, I had to do something. Then it all got out of hand."

The gun lowered to his lap.

"For what it's worth, Blackwood, I am sorry about your sister. I never intended anything to happen to her. I thought Walter was going to be alone, he should have been alone. When I saw Monica and Megan in the car with him, I didn't know what to do. I panicked, ordered him to shoot them, and he did. He shot Monica, but he wouldn't shoot Megan."

"He changed his mind later though, didn't he?" Marcus said, inching slowly across so his body was shielding Megan.

"When you sent him to England to murder a little girl because you wanted to save your own worthless skin."

"I'm sorry, I didn't know what else to do. I took the money for my wife. She's so much younger than me, you see. I needed the money for her. She likes to buy things. I know it's why she's with me, but I don't care, I had to keep her happy, had to keep her with me, so I took the money. I meant to give it back, but…"

"But you couldn't," finished Marcus. "So instead, you murdered an innocent man and his wife, my sister, and tried to kill their child."

Miles briefly closed his eyes.

"I'm sorry," he whispered again.

Marcus watched in fascination as a red dot appeared on the man's cheek.

Oblivious to it, Miles focused again on Marcus, once more pointing the gun at him.

"I had to do it," he insisted as if somehow seeking redemption from Marcus for his actions.

"Don't you see, don't you understand? No, how could you? You've always had everything you've ever wanted. I mean, look at you! You're young, rich, and handsome. You can have any woman you want – actresses, models – so many beautiful women you can take your pick of. You don't know what it's like, to know women laugh at you and are only with you for your money."

The gun wavered in his hand, and the red dot slowly crept up his face until it centred in the middle of his forehead.

"It's over," Marcus said again. "Lay down your gun. Let all of us get out of this alive."

He felt Megan stand behind him and felt her arms creep around his knees. Swiftly, he turned and lifted her into his arms.

"We're going now," he said. "And you're going to put the gun down and wait for the police."

"I can't go to prison," Miles gasped. "I won't!"

In a movement so fast Marcus barely registered it, he turned the gun under his chin and pulled the trigger.

Desperately, Marcus cradled Megan's face into his chest so she couldn't see, wouldn't have to live with the memory of...

That ... Miles, slumped in the chair, the wall behind splattered with blood and brain matter, blood spreading over the back of the chair.

Holding her to him, he left.

Left the room.

Left the house.

Left the police to clean up the mess.

~Chapter Twenty-Seven~
"We'll fix it together."

His mother's tearful relief when he walked through the door holding Megan was touching. As was the way Megan had thrown herself into her grandmother's arms, sobbing and clutching Brewster to her chest, relieved to be back with people she knew and loved.

Maybe they should relocate to New York, he thought. At least Megan would be able to see her grandmother regularly, and Marcus could adjust to life here. If Megan were happy, that would be enough.

Quietly, he told his mother what had happened, and she listened, eyes tearing up when she learnt her beloved daughter had been killed because she had been in the way.

Cuddling Megan close, she shook her head in disbelief at the desperate greed of Miles.

Slipping off his mother's lap, Megan came to him, eyes heavy with emotional exhaustion. Holding her tightly, he pulled her onto his lap as her eyelids drooped and she snuggled into his chest.

"Uncle Marcus," she mumbled around Brewster's paw.

"Yes, honey?"

"Are all the bad men gone now?"

"Yes, they're all gone now," he reassured her.

"Good." She opened her eyes and sleepily regarded him. "Please, can we go home now?"

"Home? Sweetheart, you know our apartment got all burnt up. We can't go there anymore."

"No, not there."

Almost scornful in her dismissal of the apartment, she let her eyes close and her head loll against his chest.

"Home. Home to Grace and Zoey and Finley and Connor. Please, can't we go home?"

Coming downstairs from putting Brewster and Megan down for a much-needed nap, because Brewster was so tired from all that had happened, Marcus found his mother sitting at the kitchen table, a decanter of whisky and two glasses before her.

"Isn't it a little early?" he asked.

His mother huffed at him, pouring two shots with a hand that still shook.

"Early be damned," she stated. "I think you need one, and I know I sure as hell do."

"I didn't even know you liked whisky?" he remarked, sitting down, and swallowing it in one mouthful, nodding appreciatively at the taste.

"There's a lot you don't know about me," retorted his mother, downing her shot just as fast and refilling their glasses.

"Besides, where do you think you got your taste for it? Certainly not from your father, he couldn't bear the stuff."

Marcus smiled, tipping his glass, watching the amber liquid cling to the edge. As his adrenalin subsided a headache began to pound at his temples, and he wondered if it was a good idea to have another.

"I've decided," he began. "We're going to relocate to New York, Megan, and I..."

"No, you're not," replied his mother.

"Give me one good reason why we shouldn't?"

"I can give you four. Grace and Zoey and Finley and Connor."

Marcus stared at her in shocked silence.

"So," she continued. "Are you going to tell me about them? Or do I have to drag it out of you?"

"There's not much to tell," he began.

"Good," interrupted his mother. "Then it won't take you long to tell me everything, from the beginning, without leaving out a single detail."

She eyed him beadily, her focus only slightly whisky blurred. Marcus smiled wryly at his mother's steely determination, then sighed, and looked down at his glass.

"I think I treated her very badly," he admitted slowly, shame tingeing his voice at the memory of their goodbye.

"But it was the only way, the kindest way. Otherwise, she would have thought I meant something I didn't, and I didn't, I mean I couldn't ... not about Grace, because she ... I..."

He stopped and thought about Grace, *really* thought about her. The way she looked at him, the kindness that radiated from her, her stubborn strength, and the way she would do anything to make sure her family were safe and looked after.

The hard life she had had, which far from making her bitter had instead made her open to whatever the world had to offer.

How she and her wonderful children had welcomed him and Megan into their lives, sharing with them their amazing home, making them part of their family.

Part of their family...

The sudden realisation of exactly what he had left behind, what he had thrown away, drenched him in cold, hard misery, and he choked on his whisky as a sob forced itself from his throat.

His mother laid a hand over his, waited until he finally looked up and met her eyes, and the knowing, kindly expression they contained.

"Oh, Mum," he burst out desperately, feeling like a teenager mourning his first broken heart.

"I screwed up, and I don't know how to fix it."

"So, tell me," she gently insisted. "And we'll fix it together."

They had worked hard all week. In the end, Zoey arranged for a skip to be delivered. It crouched like a pot-bellied, yellow beast in the driveway, its gaping mouth demanding to be fed, and feed it they had.

Rubbish, so much rubbish. Ten years accumulated detritus, fragments, and remnants of a life lived, of a woman who hoarded and children who created.

Hardening her heart, Zoey had bullied them into discarding so much of their past. So many memories ruthlessly sacrificed to feed the yellow beast.

Eventually, the boys got too eager in the quest to clear, and Zoey had to stop them from throwing away things that were still useful, things that might be needed. Things it would be too devastating to lose.

As they cleared, she and her mother cleaned, staying up till all hours, scrubbing, polishing, mending, and repairing, until the downstairs shone.

Gradually, the bones of the house were revealed, and their hearts broke anew at the knowledge they must leave it all behind.

That soon it would be home to Marcus and Megan, and they would have no right to it anymore.

Marcus.

Grace never mentioned him, so Zoey took her cue from her and stayed silent on the subject. She was glad to see her mother throw herself into the work, with her old grit and determination restored, but was concerned at the almost fanatical zeal behind her actions.

It was Saturday and they had stopped for lunch, all exhausted, hot, and sweaty from the mammoth task they'd undertaken, from how much they had achieved, and the thought of all they still had to do.

The doorbell sounded. Zoey and Grace exchanged weary glances. All week long, alerted by the sold sticker and the skip, neighbours had been calling around offering words of goodbye, best wishes for the future, sometimes even tears of regret.

Old Mr Branson, his face creasing at the thought of their leaving, pressed three bottles of his special elderflower champagne into Grace's hands.

Drink it in their new home, he urged her. To christen their new abode, and maybe raise a glass in memory to him.

Stunned by the generosity of their neighbours, people whose lives had been touched by her and her family, Grace felt tears well many times at the thought of going, of having to leave all of this behind.

Now, she and Zoey shared a grimace of exhaustion. Wrung out by the physical, emotional, and mental strain of dismantling their lives, neither felt able to cope with more well-wishers.

The twins ran to open the door and Grace quickly washed her hands at the sink, aware she probably had a dirty face, but unable to do anything about it.

Beside her, Zoey filled the kettle to capacity and put it on, both bracing themselves for a fresh onslaught.

"Tea?" Grace asked cheerily as she heard footsteps enter the kitchen.

"Yes, please," said a quietly familiar voice.

She turned.

He stood in the doorway, Megan by his side, looking handsome, oh so handsome, in an expensive, beautifully cut, charcoal grey suit.

He had lost weight, she thought, trying to take in the wonder of him being there, now, standing in her kitchen doorway. Yes, he had definitely lost weight.

His cheekbones, always sharply defined, were now glacial. There were dark shadows under his eyes speaking of sleepless nights and worry.

She looked tired, he thought, and sad, oh so very sad. Guiltily, he wondered if he had put such sadness in her eyes.

Glancing away, he noted the spotlessly clean condition of the kitchen. He decided it couldn't possibly be his absence that had rubbed the bloom from her skin and shaken loose the warmth from her smile. That it was much more likely the distress at losing her home that had made the weight drop from her already too skinny frame.

Neither spoke, neither could. They stood dumbly, amidst the excited chatter of the boys and Megan, as she tried to tell them the thrilling news of her kidnapping.

Of how the bad man had tried to kill her, but brave Uncle Marcus had come to get her and so the bad man had shot himself.

Trying to listen as the boys bombarded Megan for more details, and aware of Mum and Marcus simply standing there, staring at each other, Zoey decided to take matters into her own hands.

Grabbing boxes of juice from the fridge, she ushered the kids to the door.

"It sounds like Megan has an exciting story to tell us, so come on, let's go to the treehouse and she can tell us all about it there."

"But Mum ..." began Finley, or it might have been Connor.

"Can hear all about it later," Zoey promised. "Come on, out we go."

Shooting a last glance at the eerily silent adults, she pushed the reluctant twins out and closed the door behind them.

In the silence of the now deserted kitchen, they stood. Until anger flashed through her soul, and she turned away, switching the kettle back on with an annoyed snap of her hand.

"You said yes to tea?" she bit out.

He'd gone away, he'd left, treating her like a casual fling he could walk away from, making her feel worthless and so stupid to have thought, for even one moment that a man like him could ever feel anything for a woman like her.

"Tea, right." He seemed confused, uncertain of himself. He looked around in bewilderment as if unsure of his surroundings, of why he was there.

"Grace, I..."

"The surveyors have been," she broke in, determined not to let him speak, not to let him say why he was there, so afraid to hear him say those words and crush forever any hopes she may have had.

"What? Oh, right, good. Grace, I..."

"They tutted a lot, at everything," she informed him with enforced cheeriness.

"So, expect a bad report. In fact, expect them to tell you that it's a really, *really* bad idea to buy this house at all."

"But that's what I've come to tell you, Grace. That I've instructed my solicitors to withdraw the offer. That I don't want to buy the house after all."

"What?"

~Chapter Twenty-Eight~
"You are my grace, my love, my joy."

The room went cold around her, and bile rose in her throat. Unknowingly, her hands closed into fists at her side.

"*What?*" she said again.

"I'm withdrawing the offer," he repeated, his eyes never leaving her face.

"I see," she replied, her voice glacial. "May I ask why?"

"I've decided it's simply too big for me and Megan to live in alone."

"It's no bigger now than it was when you made the offer." she snapped.

"I know," he concurred. "But Grace, I..."

"What?" she snapped, then turned her back on him, shaking with fury and throwing teabags into two mugs. Grabbing a spoon from the cutlery drawer, she slammed it shut so hard it bounced back open, hitting her in the stomach.'

"Oh, fuck it!" she howled, leaning on the countertop in a winded, mindless rage. Taking deep breaths, she tried to calm herself.

"Grace." She felt him move to stand behind her. "I'm sorry, I'm not explaining myself very well. I know you must hate me right now, but please, I just wanted..."

"What? What do you want, Marcus?"

She turned to face him, horrified to feel her eyes blur at the unshed tears.

She would not cry in front of him. Would not let him see how much he had upset her.

"I'm not going to buy the house because I was kind of hoping that, in a way, you'd give it to me."

"What?"

Aware of her limited vocabulary, but unable to think of anything else to say, she stared at him in disbelief.

"You want *me* to give you, *my* house?"

"Yes, well, no. I was hoping more that you'd let Megan and I live here…"

"You want to rent my home? But not pay any bloody rent? Is that it?" Cold, hard, anger was beginning to replace her confusion now. "And where are we supposed to go?"

"No, you don't understand, I was hoping I could live here. With you." His voice rose in a futile effort to make her understand.

"As what? A bloody squatter?"

"No!"

He was yelling back now, inches away from her, his piercing blue eyes ablaze with his frustration at trying to get the right words out.

"Not as a bloody squatter, as your bloody husband!"

Wind knocked completely from her sails she sagged back against the cupboard and stared at him. Kept on staring at him until the anger left his eyes and a flush of embarrassment crept onto his face.

"Please," he said quietly. "Please, say something."

"Why?" she asked, finally.

"Because your silence is killing me."

"No, why do you want to be my ... husband?" Hardly able to say the word, Grace felt a matching blush blaze its way onto her cheeks.

"Because it makes sense. You don't want to leave your home, and we'd love to live here, but only with you here, with you all here. Without you, it would just be a house. It needs the Lovejoys in it to make it a home. Because your children, especially the boys, need a father. Because Megan needs a mother, and because she's already bonded with you, with you all."

"I see." Disappointment etched her voice in acid. "So, it's bloody convenient."

"No," he replied harshly, his eyes never leaving her face. "It's not bloody convenient. It's bloody inconvenient. I never thought, for one moment, I could fall for someone like you."

"What, a hippie?" she spat back.

"Yes, if you like, a hippie. A woman so confident about who she is, what she is, she doesn't need to wear a mask of make-up to hide from the outside world. A woman so strong, she's looked after three children totally on her own. Not only that has raised them to be the most outstandingly special people it's ever been my privilege to meet."

He paused, swallowed, and ran a trembling hand over her dreadlocks.

"Grace Lovejoy, you are the most remarkable woman I've ever come across. I went away because I didn't realise what I was leaving behind. Because I was too stupid to see, to understand that what I have been looking for all my life was right before my eyes. That a home isn't made from bricks and mortar, it's made from people. That it was you."

"Me?" she whispered wonderingly, feeling her legs shake beneath her.

"Yes, you. Perfect, amazing, beautiful you."

"I'm not beautiful."

"You are to me."

"Oh."

"You are my home, Grace. You're what I've been looking for all my life. Please ... won't you let me come home?"

Now the tears came. Hot and scalding, they leapt from her eyes to splash onto her cheeks. Trembling, she crept into his arms, felt his heart pounding wildly beneath her cheek as she lay it on his chest.

"I love you," he murmured. "God knows I've fought against it long enough, but I think I've loved you from the very first moment I saw you."

"No, you didn't," she sighed.

"Well, maybe not quite the first moment," he conceded. "After all, you made it quite plain how unimpressed you were with me, but certainly from that first evening when you tried to poison me with your wine."

He felt her laugh in his arms.

"Don't let Mr Branson hear you," she murmured. "He's given me three bottles of his elderflower champagne to toast our new home."

"We can drink it to celebrate our engagement," he promised, then pulled back and looked down at her, concern filling his expression.

"Umm, but, well, you haven't said yes to my proposal, in fact, you've not said whether you," he paused and blushed like an old-fashioned spinster in a Jane Austen novel, "return my feelings at all."

In answer, Grace pulled his head down to hers, the laughter bubbling from her mouth to his, and several, very satisfactory moments passed as she showed him, with no words necessary, exactly how she felt about him.

"I love you," she assured him when they came up for air. "Marcus Blackwood, I love you so much there aren't enough words in the English language to express it."

He smiled sheepishly, then took a small ring box from his pocket.

"I hoped, I thought, well I thought maybe, you might like this..."

Heart thudding, Grace eased the lid open on the box to reveal a pretty, old-fashioned ring. Antique, its central stone flashed with deep, swirling flames of ruby red passion.

"What is it?" she breathed, turning the box this way and that, making the flames dance within the heart of the stone.

"It's a red opal," he explained. "I looked at diamonds, but they didn't seem right. They were too cold, too sterile, they lacked ... passion. Then I saw this, and it made me think of you."

"I love it," she gasped, then handed back the box. "So, ask me then."

"I thought I already had?"

"No, you swore at me, you didn't ask."

"Oh, right, sorry."

"Do it properly now, please."

Taking the box, Marcus positioned himself on the wooden floorboards, groaning as his kneecap creaked into position.

"Grace Lovejoy, will you do me the very great honour of becoming my wife?"

"Yes," she said immediately. "Yes, yes, yes."

Slipping the ring onto her finger, Marcus thankfully scrambled back to his feet.

"It's so beautiful," she whispered, holding out her hand to admire it. "Grace Blackwood. It has a certain ring to it, don't you think?"

"No," he said, taking her into his arms. "I prefer Grace Lovejoy because you are my grace, my love, my joy."

She smiled, her eyes soft with all the love she had in her heart for him, then took him by the hand.

"Let's go home," she whispered.

"The kids?" he murmured.

"Will be fine..."

In the treehouse, the boys looked at Megan in envious admiration at her thrilling tale of kidnap, rescue, and guns.

"Wow," cried Connor, or it could have been Finley. "Just wait till Mum hears this. Let's go and tell her now."

He scrambled for the doorway, only to be pulled back by his sister who caught the back of his jumper.

"No, don't," she cautioned. "Stay here."

"Why?" he demanded. "Why can't we go and see Mum and Marcus?"

"I think," Zoey began, and smiled at Megan, who twinkled back in a shared moment of feminine conspiracy.

"I think it might be a good idea to wait until they come and get us..."

~Ten Months Later~
"You always fall so fast and so hard."

The whole family were around for Sunday lunch to celebrate his mother's arrival from the States for an extended stay, her new set of rooms finally finished to Grace's satisfaction.

Leaning back in his chair, positioned at the head of the long table, Marcus surveyed the rows of happy faces all busy chatting, drinking, and consuming the wonderful food his wife, Arianna, and Zoey had been busy cooking all morning.

His mother had deliberately not offered to help, and kept Isabella and Susannah company, claiming as none of them were kitchen goddesses, they would be better off keeping the children out of the way. But judging how much white wine had been consumed by the trio, he was suspicious of their motives.

Catching his wife's eye, he raised a brow suggestively, enjoying the blush that splashed across her cheeks. Loving the fact that after ten months of marriage, a single look was all it took to ignite that spark of passion between them.

Chuckling to himself, he took a sip of wine – Mr Branson's finest damson – and saw his mother raise a glass to him in a silent toast.

To his marriage, to his family, and to the house that now gleamed from all the love and attention that had been lavished on it over the past year. To all the restoration, renewal, and repairs that had slowly but surely revealed the beauty of the building.

Smiling at his mother, he remembered her words last year when he told her about Grace and confessed his confusion.

His conviction that as it had happened so quickly, his feelings couldn't be real, couldn't be genuine. Could they?

"You Blackwood men," she said, shaking her head in amusement. "When you fall, you always fall so fast and so hard."

Looking at his wife again, Marcus felt the warmth that always clutched his heart whenever he thought about how close he had come to leaving it all behind. To not appreciating what was right before him, – his for the taking – if only he had the sense to see it.

"So," Luke leant back in his chair in satisfaction and looked around the glory of the newly restored dining room.

"What plans do you have for the house now? Surely there's nothing left to do?"

"Well," Marcus took a sip of wine and considered. "There's the attic, we do want to convert that into a master suite for ourselves. But there's no hurry. We don't need the room we're using now for anything else so we can take our time, have a break from renovation for a bit. Maybe look at doing it next year."

At the other end of the table, Grace smiled to herself, watching her husband with his family, loving how relaxed he was, how happy they all were.

She looked around the table at his family. Her family now. Celeste, his mother. Her visits so frequent that Grace had insisted they renovate a small suite of rooms just for her, to save her having to bring so much luggage every time she flew over the ocean that separated them.

Then there was Luke, Arianna, and Lucia, and asleep upstairs, new baby Joshua. So dear to her now that she considered them her kith and kin, Lucia as close as a sister to her own brood.

The boys fidgeted in their chairs, the enforced period of good behaviour stretching them to their limits. She would tell them they could go soon, that all the children could take dessert up to the treehouse if they wished.

Then there was Zoey, her wonderful, clever daughter. She had sailed through her exams with outstanding grades, and Grace was confident her brilliant daughter had a shining future ahead of her.

Isabella had also come, and Grace was pleased to welcome her to her home. Still looking for a way to understand her tall, beautiful sister-in-law, Grace felt the woman had secrets and was intrigued by her strength and poise, wondering if she'd ever truly learn all there was to know about Isabella.

Susannah was beside her. Although they were as different as chalk and cheese, a great friendship had developed between the confident Isabella and the shy, sad Susannah.

Still alone after her divorce, Grace wished good things for her gentle sister-in-law, hoping that one day someone would come into her life and chase the shadows from her eyes.

Finally, there was Liam.

Back briefly from his assignment, he arrived on their doorstep last night, grim-faced and bearded, his eyes hinting at the horrors he had seen. Gradually, he unclenched, relaxing enough under the influence of the house to even smile now and then.

Kit, Marcus's youngest sister, had been supposed to be there as well, but a last-minute change in rehearsal scheduling had prevented her from flying over from Vienna as planned, and they were hoping she'd arrive next week.

The life of an internationally acclaimed opera singer was apparently one of constant inconvenience.

Yes, they were a close-knit and loving family, noisy in their reunions, fiercely loyal to one another, and welcoming of others who joined their ranks.

Looking about the table at the mixed clans of Blackwood, Santorini, and Lovejoy, Grace thought how lucky she and her children were to have been accepted into such a wonderful family.

Listening to her husband talk about their delayed plans for the attic, she smiled a secret smile to herself and softly stroked a hand over her stomach, wondering if now, was an appropriate occasion to inform him that in seven months' time they would be needing the extra room after all.

No, Grace decided, sipping her juice, let him enjoy this moment. There was plenty of time.

She would tell him later when they were alone...

The End...

If you have enjoyed reading

Fixtures & Fittings

Turn the page for a sneak
peek at book three of the
Blackwood Family Saga

Sugar & Spice

Where the story continues with
Susannah Blackwood

~Chapter One~
"You'll pay for that as well."

Her life was small. Susannah Blackwood paused, one hand resting on the book she had placed on the shelf. Where had that come from? She examined the idea.

True, her life was quiet, uneventful, and was concerned mostly with insular, intimate things, but small?

Small implied inconsequential, unimportant, petty. Small implied dull.

Her life was far from dull. She was busy most days running her little bookshop, a long-held childhood dream.

Okay, so maybe it wasn't the most successful bookshop in the world, but in these days of Amazon and online book retailers, it was holding its own.

She had a few close friends whom she saw occasionally, and of course, there was her family.

Her wonderful, odd, quirky family with all its steps and exes and bolt-on members. She smiled, thinking about the latest additions to the Blackwood clan.

Arianna, who had married her older brother Luke two years ago after a whirlwind and exciting courtship. With Arianna had come Lucia, her seven-year-old daughter, and now there was their new baby Josh.

And then there was Grace, her brother Marcus's bride of less than a year. Susannah's smile broadened at the thought of Grace – kind, down-to-earth, pragmatic Grace.

With her hippie dreadlocks and alternative way of living, Grace was the last person Susannah would ever have imagined her suave elder brother falling for.

A multi-millionaire businessman famed for his impeccable taste in suits and women, Marcus had had his life turned upside down when he had unexpectedly become guardian to his seven-year-old niece, Megan, after the tragic murder of Susannah's older half-sister, Monica.

Looking for a forever home for them both, he had met Grace Lovejoy and her children, the extraordinary fifteen-year-old Zoey and ten-year-old twins, Finley, and Connor.

At the thought of that naughty pair, Susannah's smile became almost a chuckle. Every week, it seemed they were in some sort of fresh trouble.

She was happy her brother had found such a wonderful, ready-made family for him and Megan, along with a magical home that he and Grace were busy restoring to its previous glory. It was an on-going project that filled their days with plans and excitement and the satisfaction of making their nest a place of beauty.

As well, they had recently announced their pregnancy and the permanent happiness in Marcus's eyes had deepened even further.

Susannah was happy for him, and Luke.

Happy they had found their soulmates. That their lives were now brimming over with love and companionship and family.

She was happy they allowed her to share in their good fortune, already loving her new nieces and nephews more than she could ever have thought possible. No, she *was* happy for them. She was. But maybe she was also a little bit jealous?

Shaking the unworthy thought from her head before it could take root, she was jolted back to the present by her phone vibrating in her pocket.

It was a text from Luke.

An appointment had cancelled, and he wondered if she was free for lunch? Naming a restaurant close to his offices, he hoped she could meet him there.

Pleased at the unexpected treat, she texted back a confirmation and they agreed a time, then she went to the front of the shop.

"Margot, I'm going out for lunch with my brother. Will you be all right alone?"

Margot, her assistant of many years, put the book she was reading down on the counter and peered over the top of her rainbow framed specs at her. Looking around the empty shop with an exaggerated gesture, she pursed her lips in thought.

"I think so. I think I'll be able to handle things."

Susannah grinned, reflecting again what a godsend Margot was and how grateful she was that she had wandered into her shop the day after it had opened five years ago and asked for a job.

She was bored, she explained. A widow of many years, her kids had all long since flown the nest and she was tired of rattling around the house by herself all day.

Taken aback at the woman's forthrightness, Susannah had stuttered out that she had only just opened, and funds were a little tight, so she hadn't planned to employ anyone yet.

"Give me a week," Margot insisted. "One week without pay as a trial period. If I don't prove my worth, then don't take me on. However, if you find you can't manage without me, then take me on part-time. My husband left me comfortably off, so I don't need much in the way of wages. I love books, and a chance to work in a bookshop is a dream come true for me."

Seeing Susannah hesitate, she added. "Go on, what have you got to lose?"

Put that way, it seemed silly to refuse, so Susannah took her on for a week's trial period. At the end of that first week, there was no question of letting Margot go, so Susannah scraped together the money for her wages and had never once regretted it.

"Go," Margot reassured. "You deserve a break, so go and have a nice lunch with your brother and make sure he pays," she said, returning to her book with a grin.

"Lord knows, he can afford it."

She was right, Luke could afford the nice things in life. Taking his share of their inheritance from their father, George Blackwood, he gambled on starting his own business ICRA, the International Child Recovery Agency. A gamble that had repaid him in spades.

Marcus, of course, had inherited the business upon their father's death and in the intervening years had seen it expand to global status, reaping its owner considerable wealth.

Susannah had used a tiny portion of her inheritance to buy the old, abandoned shop with the flat above, and renovate them both, with a view to renting out the flat to pay the running expenses of the shop beneath.

She had never imagined that a couple of years after opening the doors of Suzy's Books she would be living in the flat herself following the disintegration of her marriage.

The rest of her inheritance sat in a trust account, gathering interest, and growing daily. She could, at any time, draw upon funds to do whatever she liked – buy another shop, buy a house, travel the world – but Susannah was frugal.

Terrified of being left without money, she let it sit, viewing it as her retirement plan, a back-up to compensate for a life spent alone.

After the loss of Matt and her marriage, Susannah was too shattered to even consider pursuing another relationship.

Even though she had the examples of her own brothers' blissfully happy marriages, she firmly believed she had had her chance at that with Matt and she had blown it.

Now, as she travelled up in the elevator to Luke's suite of offices with her belly comfortably full of a wonderful meal and a couple of glasses of rose wine, Susannah sighed in contentment and leant against Luke's shoulder.

He looked down at her in amusement.

"Bit squiffy? Too much wine?"

She shook her head. "No, just happy. Thank you, it was a gorgeous lunch; that restaurant is amazing."

"I know, but I'm not sure it's good it's so close to the office." Ruefully Luke patted his toned, muscled stomach. "Too many corporate lunches and I'll be needing to hit the gym a bit more."

The doors slid open, and the large, open-plan office was revealed. Dozens of agents were working at consoles and talking on phones, tracking down leads and making enquiries.

ICRA were renowned worldwide for an almost one hundred percent success rate at retrieving missing children. Be they kidnapped or snatched by a parent, the worldwide network ICRA commanded could search under any stone and not stop until the child had been recovered.

Making their way to Luke's office, Susannah smiled hello at one of the operatives slouched in front of a screen, his face screwed up into a comical expression of distaste.

"Hi, James," she said.

"Oh, hey Susannah."

James Sullivan crinkled a smile, his deep brown eyes lighting up with genuine pleasure at seeing her.

Straightening in his chair, his large frame and long legs making desk work torture, he pushed his dreadlocks over his shoulder, a large finger scratching at a caramel-coloured cheekbone.

"You okay?" she asked.

"Nope," he replied, and Luke laughed.

"Jimmy Sullivan," he announced, gesturing to his employee. "One of my best operatives in the field, one of my worst at filling out his paperwork. Desk, five minutes," he ordered with a grin, and Sullivan snapped a salute.

"Boss," he acknowledged.

Still smiling, Susannah followed her brother into his glass-walled office.

"Now," Luke said, unlocking a drawer and pulling out a flat, green jeweller's box. "What do you think of this?"

This was a gorgeous necklace of jade and silver with a large, heart-shaped pendant of jade that glowed warmly in the afternoon sun streaming through the floor to ceiling windows.

"It's beautiful," Susannah gasped. Dropping her scarf and bag on a chair she reached out to gently stroke it. Lifting it in her hand, she was surprised at its weight, loving the way it fitted into her palm.

"Arianna is going to love it. It perfectly matches those jade earrings she always wears."

"I know," Luke was grinning with anticipated pleasure. "Took me ages to find the exact match. I managed to smuggle the earrings out of the house while she was out for the day with Isabella and Grace. My jeweller examined them and took detailed photos and I had them back in her jewellery box before she got back."

"Is everything ready for the party?" Susannah murmured, still distracted by the perfection of the pendant.

"Yep, it's all set. You're still coming, aren't you?" he enquired anxiously.

"Of course." Susannah flashed him a reassuring smile. "I wouldn't miss it for the world. Speaking of which." She glanced at her watch.

"Margot told me to take the rest of the day off and have fun, so I think I'm going to hit Oxford Street and treat myself to something new to wear to the party."

"You do that," Luke ordered, gently packing the pendant back into its box and securely locking it away again in the drawer.

Susannah picked up her bag, relaxing into her brother as he came around the desk and gathered her up in a bear hug.

"Thank you for lunch," she mumbled into his shirt.

"You're welcome," he replied into her hair. "Now, go shop, have fun, and we'll see you at the restaurant on Saturday. Don't forget, everyone is to be there for seven."

"I know," she pulled herself free and headed for the door. "See you then. Oh, hi James," she held the door open so Sullivan could enter, triumphantly brandishing his completed paperwork.

"Bye James," she finished, and he flashed a perfect, white smile at her.

"Bye Susannah." Closing the door behind her, he dropped the file onto Luke's desk.

"Done," he declared.

Luke shook his head in wry amusement at Sullivan's well-known hatred of paperwork and all things office bound.

"Did Susannah leave this?" Sullivan asked, picking up a soft, paisley patterned scarf from the chair.

"Damn, wonder if I can still catch her!"

"It's okay," Sullivan tucked the scarf into his jacket pocket. "I'm now going, so I'll probably catch up with her downstairs."

Letting herself out into the street, Susannah realised she should have phoned for a taxi from Luke's office. The block where Luke's offices were located were tucked away in an isolated side street near the river so her chances of hailing one, were minimal.

For a second, she considered going back up, but it was a glorious day, and she knew that a quick, five-minute walk would soon have her on the main thoroughfare where taxis passed by regularly.

Shouldering her bag, she tipped her head to the sun, closing her eyes in appreciation of its warmth.

A hand, large and strong, slapped over her shocked mouth, silencing the automatic scream, and she froze in fear as she was dragged backwards into one of the many small alleys that wound away down to the river.

Regaining her senses, Susannah struggled desperately, catching a glimpse of her assailant. Cold blue eyes stared into hers, a thin mouth quirking in amusement at her futile struggles.

His arms were like bands of unbreakable steel as he pulled her further into the gloom between the overhanging buildings.

Heart hammering with fear, Susannah realised this man meant to seriously hurt her, and she tried to fight back, lashing out with a steel-tipped heel at his shin.

He yelped in pain and the hand on her mouth relaxed.

She bit him, as hard as she could. Recoiling in disgust from the acrid taste of nicotine tainted flesh, she screamed, once, and then the hand was clamped tightly over her mouth again.

"Bitch," he whispered into her ear. "You'll pay for that as well."

Terror swallowed her whole at his words.

SUGAR & SPICE

Amazon

eBook ~ paperback ~
free to read on Kindle Unlimited

~About the Author~

Julia Blake lives in the beautiful historical town of Bury St. Edmunds, deep in the heart of the county of Suffolk in the UK, with her daughter, one crazy cat, and a succession of even crazier lodgers.

Her first novel, The Book of Eve, met with worldwide critical acclaim, and since then, Julia has released many other books which have delighted her growing number of readers with their strong plots and instantly relatable characters. Details of all Julia's novels can be found on the next page.

Julia leads a busy life, juggling working and family commitments with her writing, and has a strong internet presence, loving the close-knit and supportive community of fellow authors she has found on social media and promises there are plenty more books in the pipeline.

Julia says: "I write the kind of books I like to read myself, warm and engaging novels, with strong, three-dimensional characters you can connect with."

~ *A Note from Julia* ~

If you have enjoyed this book, why not take a few moments to leave a review on Amazon,

It needn't be much, just a few lines saying you liked the book and why, yet it can make a world of difference.

Reviews are the reader's way of letting the author know they enjoyed their book, and of letting other readers know the book is an enjoyable read and why. It also informs Amazon that this is a book worth promoting, and the more reviews a book receives, the more Amazon will recommend it to other readers.

I would be very grateful and would like to say thank you for reading my book and if you do spare a few minutes of your time to review it, I do see, read, and appreciate every single review left for me.

Best Regards
Julia Blake

~ *Other Books by the Author* ~

The Blackwood Family Saga

Fast-paced and heart-warming, this exciting series tells the story of the Blackwood Family and their search for love and happiness

The Perennials Series

Becoming Lili – the beautiful, coming of age saga
Chaining Daisy – its gripping sequel
Rambling Rose – the triumphant conclusion

The Book of Eve

A story of love, betrayal, and bitter secrets that threaten to rip a young woman's life apart

Black Ice

An exciting steampunk retelling of the Snow White fairy tale

The Forest ~ a tale of old magic ~

Myth, folklore, and magic combine in this engrossing tale of a forgotten village and an ancient curse

Erinsmore

A wonderful tale of an enchanted land of sword and sorcery, myth and magic, dragons, and prophecy

Eclairs for Tea and Other Stories

A fun collection of short stories and quirky poems that reflect the author's multi-genre versatility